Storm Season

Jan Dawson

Library of Congress Control Number: 2023909631

ISBN 979-8-218-20874-5
Ebook ISBN 979-8-218-21630-6

Dedication

For Dave

About This Book

One island. Two hurricanes. And a love separated by decades.

A woman yearns to be free from the memories of the man who disappeared after a violent hurricane devastated her island decades ago. Now when a second storm creates chaos on the island, she is stunned to learn that he might be back. But is there room in her heart to forgive him for abandoning her or will she lose this second chance at real love?

Susan Kent is shaken to her core. Years ago, she placed Chris deep into the recesses of her mind. Then her granddaughter swears she has met him and Susan is forced to come to grips with powerful, conflicting emotions of love and anger.

Watching her daughter and granddaughter work through their own emotional chaos with Chris, Susan struggles to accept this cataclysmic change in their family. And when Chris, who desperately wants to reconcile, appears to question her loyalty, she draws an absolute line in the sand.

Will Susan and Chris be able to acknowledge their true

feelings, or will they lose their chance at love, this time forever?

Storm Season, a stand-alone novel, is a sweet romance. If you love stories about true love lost then found later in life, resolving family conflict, and pathways to emotional healing, you'll adore this moving happily-ever- after tale of life on a sandbar.

Prologue

The Year 1975

Susan stretched out her legs on the old rocking chair and took a deep breath. She couldn't see too much of the ocean over the railing and across the street, but what she could see did seem to look a bit rougher than it had this afternoon. Or was that just her imagination?

It had been a very busy day; unexpected in that yesterday, Thursday, no one seemed to be overly concerned about the storm that was somewhere in the Gulf Stream off the coast of Georgia. But overnight, the idea that it might just veer off to the east seemed to diminish, and now there was concern for the North Carolina Coast. No one was thinking about a direct hit, but if it came close enough, the tides would be a huge nuisance.

She had arrived at the motel office that morning to the sound of the phone ringing and had to scramble to answer before the caller hung up.

"Hey Susan, it's Annie," said the voice on the phone.

"Annie, it's early for you. What's up? You sound out of breath," asked Susan.

"Just got a call from the district office and all of us seasonal employees have to evacuate," she replied. "Just thought you should know."

Annie was from Pittsburgh, down for a summer season with the National Park Service. They'd become friends over the course of the summer as Susan occasionally ran into her on beach patrols. This evacuation order meant that someone somewhere thought this storm might be a bit more than a glancing blow.

"Thanks so much, Annie. I'm sure you'll be back tomorrow, so have fun doing whatever you do when you evacuate," Susan laughed.

"I will," Annie responded. "But maybe you should check in with your folks to see if they want you to take any special precautions. It wouldn't hurt."

"I hate to bother them, but you're probably right," Susan admitted. "See ya then. And thanks again. Bye"

They rung off, and Susan hesitated for a moment before calling her parents to get their take on things. They were off the island most of the summer in Richmond taking care of her grandmother, and had given her the chance as a nine-teen-year-old college student to manage the Hatteras Hideaway Motel for the summer. It had been an uneventful summer up to this point. The weather had been good all summer long. The guests seemed happy to be on the island, and she'd had plenty of free time for walks along the beach to observe and study the tides and the marine life, which fit perfectly into her Marine Biology major at the University of North Carolina in Wilmington. She had garnered a huge collection of shells, and was quite proud of the Scotch Bonnets she had lined up on the porch railing at home.

"What should I do, Dad?" Susan asked. She relayed Annie's message and also told him she noted everyone was already busy with storm preparations when she peddled to the motel at half past seven that morning.

"I don't think you need to worry too much," her dad replied. "From what I can tell, this storm will move off from the Cape and you might get a bit of wind and some small issues with storm tide, but other than that, not too much. How many guests do we have right now?"

Susan didn't need to look at the reservation book. "Three reservations which wrap up Saturday. Two older couples who are repeat customers and one family with small children," she replied. She reflected silently that the low number was one good thing. As it was into August, things had started to wind down. Labor Day was still a ways away. "Do I need to tell them to leave?"

"Probably wouldn't hurt. I know they'll be disappointed, but they would be leaving tomorrow anyway, so hopefully it won't be an issue. You can give them their money back for the one night or maybe they'll take a credit on a future reservation. If two of them are repeats, they must like us," her dad chuckled. "But seriously, since the Park Service seems concerned enough to evacuate staff, I'd clear out the motel, and then have Scott do the usual storm prep. Have the cleaners get those rooms in order so that tomorrow, when the new visitors arrive, it will be all good."

"OK," Susan sighed. "I'll try to catch these folks now to give them time to pack up. I have your 'storm to-do list' on the tack board, so I'll be sure to check everything off. Don't worry, but I'd better get going. Give Grandma my love and same to Mom." She'd ended the call then, mindful of the long-distance charges. No need to talk at length. She'd tried to make sure the motel made money during her stint as Manager.

Scott, the maintenance man, was driving up as she hung up the phone. She stepped outside onto the porch and called out to him. "Scott, Dad says I've got to tell our guests to leave and you need to tape up the windows and do anything else you need to do for this storm."

Scott looked up and nodded. "If he hadn't told you, I was gonna," he said. "My barometer is falling a little too fast for my likin'. And every place I passed drivin' here was taping and boarding and moving stuff up and out of the way. I guess it's better to be safe than sorry, huh?"

Susan nodded, hollered out, "Thanks," and went back inside the office. The older folks swore by their barometers. They knew plenty about what the weather was going to do before the forecasters did. She had plenty to do as well, but the first thing was to talk to the guests and give them the bad news. The couple with the small children was easy to convince. Apparently, the kids had been a handful all week and had more than their share of sun and sand. Since the family lived in Richmond, they didn't have a long drive. The older couples were not as easy to deal with, claiming it was much ado about nothing. But after promising them a night's refund and reminding them about what salt water could do to their car, they agreed to head home. By about one that afternoon the parking lot was empty and Susan moved onto other things.

Working with the housekeepers, she got all of the rocking chairs off the porches and helped Scott tape up the doorknobs to keep the salt water and sand out. There were a few umbrellas and chairs left by previous guests that needed to be placed in the storage room, and she stacked all the chairs on top of one another by the pool to keep them from flying around. Periodically, she stopped to look up at the sky. *No indication of anything being amiss today*, she thought. It was a gorgeous day with a light breeze and blue skies, albeit with some clouds gathering on the horizon. Maybe the weather radio people had it all wrong. It wouldn't be the first time. But like Scott had said, "Better safe than sorry," so here they were, all over the island, shooing away visitors, taping windows, stashing away loose items and looking at the sky.

Yes, it had been a busy day. As Susan stretched out even further on the rocker and let her muscles relax, the resident motel cat, High Tide, jumped on her lap.

"What do you think, High Tide?" she asked. The cat lazily flicked its tail and began purring. "Guess you're not too worried, so I won't be either."

She closed her eyes and reflected again on how well the summer had gone. And it wasn't just from the motel's perspective. It had been fun in other ways. There were young people her age, some a bit younger, and some a bit older, all over the island. Summer help, vacationers, and a few of the locals had managed to find each other and make the most of the long summer days and warm starry nights. Every night, it seemed someone had a bonfire. There was beer, sometimes a bit of alcohol someone had pilfered from somewhere, guitar music, and casual sex. Romances came

5

and went with the tide. She hadn't given in yet, but when she thought of Chris, she knew she would if she ever had the chance.

Chris was from somewhere up north, no one was sure where – Baltimore? He was the first mate on the SeaAnna, Captain Terry Neal's boat, the best boat in the fleet, word had it. Chris had a reputation of being good with the guests, great with the boat, and a lot of fun in general. Captain Neal was very picky about whom he kept on as a mate, she'd heard, so apparently, Chris has passed the test. But also, he was amazingly good looking. Tall, tanned, and in great shape from his work on the boat, with bleached hair and a grin that seemed to extend from one end of the Pamlico sound to the other, he made her catch her breath any time she was around him. Could she find a way to be around him more before the summer ended?

"Hey, sleeping beauty, you'd best finish up whatever you need to do in the office and then get home and take care of stuff there," Scott called.

Susan jerked up and High Tide scampered off her lap. "I just was resting my eyes, Scott," she said just a bit defensively. "I'm kinda worn out."

"You and me both," he replied. "But I think everything is in order now, so I'm headed on home to Miss Maggie to be sure we got our place all tied down."

"Oh, Scott, thank you for everything," she called out. "I really do appreciate it and I know Mom and Dad do too. You give Miss Maggie my love."

"Do you need a ride to your place?" he queried.

"No, I have my bike, and it's so close. But thanks anyway."

"Just be sure to put that bike inside tonight and don't be leavin' it under the house. Tide at best will kill it with salt and at worse it will wash away. I don't know what's in store, but as the day's gone on, I'm just feelin' a bit uneasy. And the barometer doesn't lie."

Susan laughed. "I'll be sure to take care of the bike. You go on now, and I will see you tomorrow." She waved as Scott nodded, got into his car, and headed off. She walked back to the office, took a look around, and as an afterthought, grabbed the reservation book and the cash box and locked the door behind her. Only then did she realize she'd left the rocking chair on the porch. She turned it on its side, then pushed it up against the building. *This will have to do,* she thought and then said aloud to High Tide who was nowhere in sight, "If things get too rough tonight, High Tide, just crawl in here, and I'll see you in the morning too."

She carried the book and the box down the steps off the porch and placed them in the basket on her bike. She felt the wind in her face as she hopped on for the short ride home. She passed the two other motels located on the beach, all quiet and taped up as well. She was surprised at how little traffic there was, especially for a Friday night. *People must be taking this pretty seriously,* she thought.

She waved to Matt at Matt's Friendly Grocery as she turned down the path to her home. "You take care, Mr. Matt," she hollered. His front display glass had a huge "X" taped across it, the universal sign of an impending storm.

"You too," he waved. "I'm staying open a bit later this evening 'til folks get what they need, but I'm about out of bread and milk. You need anything?"

"Nah, I'm good, but thank you. See you tomorrow," she called out over her shoulder as he disappeared from her view and she pulled into her drive. She looked up at the steps and, for just a moment, thought about leaving the bike underneath the house. But since it was her only means of transportation with her parents having the car, she thought better of it and lugged it up to the landing, reservation book and cash box and all. She opened the door and stuck the bike and its contents inside, and then took all the plants and shells off the porch railings and brought them inside too. She checked her mom's infamous 'Storm Drawer' to get flashlights and fresh batteries, and she pulled the weather radio from the top shelf in the kitchen and put in fresh batteries there too, just in case.

Only then did she notice that she could hear the surf pounding, which was rare because she lived a good way from the oceanfront. She glanced out the window and saw an unbelievably gorgeous sunset, with purples, pinks, and an unsettling blood red color on the horizon. And there was a whistling sound, ever so softly, but persistently, that she wasn't sure she'd ever heard before. The lights flickered for just a moment, and despite the warmth of the evening, Susan shivered.

Chapter One

Present Day

Susan stretched out her legs on the old rocking chair and took a deep breath. The current cat-in-residence, Low Tide, hopped up on the porch railing and looked warily at her.

"What are you thinking, Low Tide?" Susan asked out loud. "In your cat family memory, are you thinking back like I am, back to seventy five? Your great-great-great grandmother High Tide must have had one heck of a night that night. I remember finding her soaking wet and shaking like a leaf on the porch that next morning with no sign of that old rocking chair I had turned over to protect her. In fact, not much of the porch was left either."

Low Tide only sat there, quietly, giving nothing away. Susan looked past her and out to the edge of the beach, which now, after so many years, was unfortunately clearly visible from the porch. The swell was definitely increasing and there was no question this time around that they were in for a bad storm. No need to guess with a barometer or achy joints. The Weather Channel had been all over this one since it was a wave coming off Africa. The first for the Cape Verde season, and it was headed for the North Carolina coast.

It was uncanny, she thought, that this storm, now christened Eva, was taking the same track, coming at the same time in mid-August, and was starting with the same letter as Hurricane Evelyn had done all those years ago. Halfway hypnotized by the crashing sounds of the waves, her thoughts drifted back to Evelyn, and as always, to Chris. Chris who had been there for her from the time the storm blew away up the coast to the time he seemed to blow out of her life. She thought of him making his way through the tide to the house the morning after, helping her navigate her way to the motel through the salt water, sand, and debris. How he held her when she saw the devastation, how he vowed to help her organize the cleanup, and how he was there every moment he could spare from cleaning up the harbor, which was left a mangled pile of what had been fine fishing boats. The way of life for so many of their friends was destroyed overnight.

But then, her thoughts went to those nights after cleanup, when there was nothing more to do for the day. When the blood, sweat, and tears had all been expended for the time being, and they had just each other to commiserate with, and more importantly, to hold onto. With no power at first, it was too hot to stay inside anywhere, and the mosquitoes were bad everywhere except right along the oceanfront. That was their escape. There had been a first time, and then there were more. And in the confusion and chaos of those days after the hurricane, she had forgotten her pill. Maybe once? Maybe twice? It really didn't matter because she wasn't thinking of that at the time. Just always counting on Chris to be there and to make everything seem like it would be OK in the end. She could almost feel his touch, his lips, his strength, and hear his reassurances. Her shoulders sagged a bit with the weight of the memories, tears gathering at the corner of her eyes.

"Gran, we really need to get going."

She heard the voice like from a dream. "Were you asleep, Gran?" asked her granddaughter Jo. "I know you worked way too hard today. You know we still have time to get off the island but that window is closing fast. We'd have to leave soon because they are going to close the Basnight Bridge in about two hours. We need to pack and then get on the road and..."

"JoBell Leonard, we are not going to evacuate and that's that," Susan pronounced. "You know as well as I do that our presence would only be an imposition on your mom and dad, and I don't need that discomfort or drama right now. I will be here for the motel just like I was before. The house is strong, we have the generator now, and I am not leaving. Pure and simple." Her hard demeanor softened a bit. After a tired sigh, she added, "But I wouldn't blame you for going, so don't let my stubbornness stop you, OK?"

Jo looked at her grandmother and saw in her everything she hoped she could become – strong and independent, and yet caring and understanding. These were supposed to be her golden years.

Her mother and grandmother had become estranged. Why that had happened was such a tangle she wasn't sure it could ever be sorted out. But those same feelings seemed to apply to her and her mother as well, so she was in no way anxious to drive to Raleigh to be with her parents and be subjected to what she felt was their constant criticism of her and also of her grandmother.

"No, Gran. I'm staying here with you for all the same reasons you just said. We'll be fine. You've been through this before and now you have me. And Dare too. And speaking of Dare, he said if we didn't evacuate, he'd meet us at the Frisco Airport around half past six so that we can drop off the car and he'd drive us back and help us put any last minute stuff in the shed. It was great that you had him raise that shed last year. Hopefully, the sound tide won't come up that far. Let me call him and tell him we'll meet him there."

Susan watched Jo carefully as she spoke of Dare. She wondered what the level of feeling was there between them. Jo only saw him when she would come by from school on breaks, or during the summers. They had known one another since they were kids, when Susan would drive to Raleigh to collect her and bring her for her annual month-long visit. How she and Jo both looked forward to that time, how they shared their mutual love of the ocean and the coast, and how they were always sad when it was time to leave. And Jo had met Dare Davis, the local boy, and their friendship, or whatever it was, had seemed to stand the test of time and frequent separations.

"Dare is a real sweetheart, Jo," Susan replied. "And I will always be grateful for that work he did on the shed. But you know he comes around even when you're not here to check on me when he can. He'll pop into the motel on days when he can't go out fishing, and when he does fish, he almost always brings me a little something."

Jo grabbed her hair and re-did her ponytail in the wind.

Working at the motel for the summer had been good for her. She'd shed the freshman fifteen she'd put on her first year at school, and she'd actually gotten fairly toned from the physical work she was doing, from cleaning the occasional room to hauling laundry back and forth for guests who required extra towels or bedding, to sweeping the sand that constantly blew onto the porches and stairs. She was bright and engaging and the guests loved her. She had a smile that reminded Susan of Chris. But Jo didn't know that.

"Let's get that rocker inside and lock up," Jo said, saying nothing more about Dare. "I remember you telling me about the rocker you left out for High Tide and that story did not have a good ending, so there's one lesson learned from nineteen seventy-five."

Susan laughed as they lugged the heavy rocker inside, and took one last look around the office.

"I debated on bringing the computers and stuff with us," said Jo, "but with everything available on my phone, it won't matter. Plus, from what they say, we'll lose cell service, so it's kind of silly to bother."

Susan nodded as they got into her car, letting Jo drive as she often did these days. She glanced back as they pulled out onto the highway and wondered thoughtfully about what they'd find in the morning. The wind was beginning to pick up and shift, and clouds were already building on the horizon.

"You've listened to the Weather Channel more than I have today," said Susan. "What's the latest?"

"Cat two bordering on three." Jo sighed. "It's not going to be pretty. Of course, you never know how much sound tide there will be, but for sure our beach is going to take a hit, and then there's the wind. You would know more than me what to expect."

"Well, they say Evelyn was a strong two, so if this is worse, it's going to be rough. And to think during Evelyn, I thought we'd be back in business in a day. It sure didn't work out that way."

Susan lapsed into silence as they drove to the airport, the highest point on the island.

Turning into the airport entrance, Jo exclaimed, "You'd think people were here to board planes to evacuate, instead of just parking their cars. Look at all this traffic! We'll have to go pretty far along to find a space. Guess people have been bringing vehicles here all day."

Sure enough, they were almost to the campground entrance past the airport when they found a spot, and Dare was, as promised, waiting for them.

"How in the world did you know we'd be parking right here?" Jo asked.

"Pretty easy," Dare grinned. "I knew it would be packed, and coming at this time I just kept driving until I figured this is where you'd have to stop. I think everyone from Buxton south has parked here. There was no one even at the Baptist Church lot and that's usually packed."

"The sound tide would have to be something to get to the church," Susan shook her head. "But with what they are predicting, I guess no one wants to take chances."

Dare looked carefully at Susan, her gray hair now flying about her face with the increasing wind. "Miss Susan, I hope you made the right decision to stay. You and Jo both. The talk at the docks today has been the most concerned I've ever heard. I'll try to keep up with you as much as I can tonight, but who knows how long the cell towers will hold up if we get the wind they're predicting. I'll be staying with Mom and Dad, at least it's a bit of higher ground there and in the woods."

"It's a bit late for me to worry about my decision now, Dare," Susan answered. "But let's get on so that you can get us home and then you get onto your folks' place." She smiled at him fondly. "I'm glad you're going there. Your little place at the docks? Well, probably not the safest."

"Agreed," nodded Dare. They were quiet as they returned to the highway. Traffic was all but non-existent with people either already home or off the island. Susan realized she no longer saw windows covered with "Xs" as they had been during Evelyn. That method of saving windows had been proven not to work very well. Instead, there were plywood panels on windows and doors everywhere with messages to Hurricane Eva, advising her to "Leava" or other such silly sentiments. *If only that could be the case*, Susan thought wistfully.

"I really think we've got everything covered, Dare," said Susan as they pulled up to her house. "Jo and I put all the shells and plants and yard tools and what-not in the shed last night. And her bike and whatever else we thought might fly around."

Dare scanned the property under the house and took a quick glance up at the porch railings. "Looks like it," he agreed. "Then I will head on out. Please take care, OK?" He gave Susan a quick hug and turned to Jo. "I mean it, call me if you need anything, Jo. Don't be a hero. Please."

Jo shrugged and then smiled. "I won't. I've got Gran to

look after and I take that responsibility seriously. You take care too." She walked over and gave him a hug and a quick peck on the cheek. "And thanks for everything."

They both waved as he drove away and then climbed up the steps and stood on the porch looking at the sun just beginning to go into full sunset mode.

"Those colors are weird, Gran," said Jo. "Was it like that with Evelyn?"

"Unfortunately, yes. Very similar," Susan responded as she took in the purples, pinks, and reds. "Never thought I'd see that kind of sky again, but here we are."

"You know, Gran," said Jo as she unlocked the door and they walked into the house together. "You've never really told me about how it was with Hurricane Evelyn, and how you coped afterward, and you know, what happened after that with Mom. She added almost shyly, "She says she never asked you. That she didn't want to hear it."

"That's true," sighed Susan. "And I'm not sure you need to hear it either, but you have asked, and so maybe it's only fair that you know what happened. All of what happened. And why things turned out the way they did. You're old enough for sure." Looking out the window, she stated, "It's not an easy story for me to tell, so let's get some dinner first and get settled in for the night ahead."

Jo nodded and flipped on the television just as the announcer intoned, "This storm is strengthening by the hour and we can only hope folks evacuated or have a solid storm plan in place. We'll keep you informed with live coverage throughout the ..."

Jo flipped off the station. "I guess we'll find out soon enough. No need to hear it over and over."

But Susan didn't reply. She was still looking at the sunset, and felt that same chill settle over her.

Chapter Two

They worked together to finish washing and drying the few dishes they'd used for supper, neither one having had much appetite.

"I hear that whining sound you always mentioned," remarked Jo as she put up the last glass into the cupboard. "It really is annoying."

"It will be with us now for the duration," said Susan. "It about drove me crazy during Evelyn. It just won't stop."

"Well, maybe if we keep ourselves occupied with stimulating conversation, we won't notice so much," said Jo. "You did say you would tell me about the other storm and you know," she shrugged, "about Mom and all. You don't have to tell me things that make you sad or anything, but I am trying to understand it all."

All of it makes me sad, thought Susan.

"Let's re-arrange these couches against the wall so that we can make ourselves a bit of a cave to stay in," she said. "And once we're settled, I'll try to tell you what you want to know."

"You know," said Jo as they pushed the couches around and set the pillows up like children making an imaginary fort. "One thing I don't understand from the very start is why people weren't more prepared. For Evelyn, I mean. It's not like there weren't storms before."

"Well, we were prepared, at least as far as we could be," Susan began. "You have to understand that there hadn't been a storm that bad in a number of years, and so, for younger folks, we didn't have those memories. But we also didn't have the technology or the communication tools we all rely on today." Susan glanced over at her new flat screen TV. "There was very little television reception on the island." She wished there was an easier way to make her granddaughter understand.

"Remember, back then we didn't have cable. You had to stick tin foil on the top of the TV's antenna, and that's assuming you even had a TV."

Jo shook her head in disbelief and laughed a little.

"Sounds impossible, right?" She tried lightening the mood a bit, but the weight on her chest was too heavy. "But like I said, there weren't too many TVs around. The reception was horrible because the nearest stations, like Norfolk, were too far away, and what with wind and all, you couldn't see much half the time. And satellites to track storms were in their infancy. And, of course, to top it off, there was no Weather Channel." Susan stopped as if to look back into time and a nostalgic smile found its way to her lips. "People relied on their local knowledge, which to tell the truth was pretty darn good. The fishermen could read the wind and the tides and the currents, and even the clouds. They knew something was up. And I mean, we did have radios and so we'd heard it was coming." Susan shrugged recalling the memories. "We all did what we could to board up, tape up, and hunker down. It's just, well, it was crazy bad." She shook her head. "Later, we learned the track went right over us, so we got both sides. And if what we heard today was correct, we'll get the same thing tonight. And the backside is way worse." She shivered slightly, remembering that night. "Way worse."

"After the eye passes, right?" asked Jo. "I mean, that's all you hear about now is how weird the eye is." Jo suddenly sat up straight as she thought about what that eye might mean for the two of them. "I know, I am going to get your old air mattress and we'll stick it down here between the couch and the wall. I think you and I can share the mattress. We don't have a lowest space and we don't have any interior rooms so I guess this wall is going to have to do." Looking around as she got up, she added, "At least we're away from the windows."

Once Jo found the mattress, inflated it, and got it into position, she and Susan squeezed into their makeshift bunker for the night.

"So, what was it like? Where did you stay?" asked Jo.

"I stayed up for quite a while just watching the lightning flashing in the distance. The rain came and went. Those were the rain bands of course. But then the lightning and thunder got to be so bad and the rain was just pounding

19

on the roof." Susan glanced at Jo who seemed transfixed by her grandmother's story. "I got scared and, you're going to laugh at this, I hid under my bed, and I stayed there until first light." She shrugged.

"Really?" Jo was looking at her with a mixture of skepticism and awe.

"Yes. And this house shook like you wouldn't believe, so get ready for that, and I didn't think I had slept at all but I must have slept a bit because I don't actually recall the quiet of the eye." Susan paused and looked Jo straight in the eye. "But when that backside hit, I thought for sure the house would just splinter into a million pieces." She rubbed her own arms as if trying to warm herself. "There was just that whistling of the wind. That's what I remember the most about that night."

"And what about the next morning?" Jo asked. She was trying her best not to think about the fact that she would have to go through all this herself within a few hours. *Be calm*, she thought. *If Gran did this and survived, so can you.*

"It was a nightmare, Jo," Susan admitted. "Looking out the window, all I could see was water. We were all in water. The wind was still blowing, but believe it or not, there were peeks of sunshine, and that just seemed to make it surreal. We were all these little islands of houses in this beautiful morning light, but it was all wrong." Susan stood up and looked toward her living room window on the other side of where they had bunkered down. "There were places I could see through where there should have been trees but the trees were gone. And I could see smoke and I thought that was weird." Susan sat down again and placed her head in her hands. "Oh Jo, it was so sad. It was Matt's Friendly Grocery. It was located where the "Big One" tackle shop is now. Mr. Matt was the nicest man. And something shorted and the store caught fire and was destroyed." Susan stopped for a moment and Jo sensed her sadness about something that happened all those years ago. "It destroyed Mr. Matt too. He had a heart attack just about six months later, and then it was not long after he passed away. He didn't have insurance to rebuild the store and he seemed to lose his way in life after that." Susan paused again and tilted her head to one side. "You know, Jo? Hurricanes can do more than destroy beaches and buildings and lives. For the survivors, they'll destroy your soul if you let them. I really believe that's what happened to him. You would have liked him a lot. He was a good man."

Susan paused and Jo stayed quiet for a few moments, allowing her grandmother to collect her thoughts. She knew the story was actually just beginning.

"And so, you didn't stay in the house all day, did you, Gran?"

"No, of course not. I tried calling my mom and dad in Richmond, knowing they'd be beside themselves, but there was no dial tone." Susan sounded matter-of-factly now. "It was a few hours before I felt like it was safe enough to venture out, and about the time I had my boots on and was ready to leave, I saw someone making their way toward the house." Susan winced and Jo looked at her grandmother carefully. "It was Chris, a guy I knew from our group of friends that summer. I really had a crush on him as we said back then. I suppose you'd say I thought he was hot. But I always had admired him from afar. I mean, we spoke and all, but he was the last person I expected to see coming up the drive that morning."

"Chris," Jo said softly. "Chris what? Where was he from?"

"Chris Smith. How common a name is that?" Susan

responded, shaking her head slightly. "And you know, I don't know where he was from. Just somewhere "up North" as we all used to say. Someone had said maybe from around Baltimore or DC." Susan shrugged, then continued matter-of-factly. "It really didn't concern any of us who were working and living at the beach for the summer where we were from. It was a time to have fun and meet people and enjoy life in that moment. We didn't have phones or computers or much of anything else to amuse us. We lived for our time off from whatever jobs we had just to soak up the sun and enjoy life. It was all pretty simple, until it all got complicated."

"And so, this Chris just magically appears at your door step after Hurricane Evelyn and creates havoc?" Jo asked. "Doesn't make sense, or am I missing something?"

"I guess I was too naïve to realize he was interested in me too," Susan said. "I was honestly stunned. He had surveyed the damage at the harbor and then he and a friend grabbed the friend's old beater truck and drove up as far as they could. When the water got too high, they left the truck and just walked, taking it all in."

Jo could hardly breathe, she was so caught up in her grandmother's sharing. Susan went on. "His friend went one way and he told him he'd catch up with him by the motels and that he was coming for me. He called from the driveway to ask if I was OK, and he said he'd walk with me to the motel if I wanted to go." Susan looked at Jo and smiled wistfully. "I remember walking down the steps from the porch and thinking it was almost too much to take in – the storm, the water, and then Chris. I was probably in a bit of a state of shock, but for sure I fell apart when we got to the motel."

She paused then as if coming up for air after a deep

dive. "Jo, I have some wine in the fridge, and if you don't mind, I'm going to have some. And I know you're not twenty-one yet but I also know you've sampled wine before, so if you 'd like some, bring us some glasses."

Jo nodded and climbed out of their pillow reinforcements.

So, his name was Chris. At least that was something. But how did it get to – her thought was interrupted by a huge blast of wind. The house shook and the lights flickered. She poured the wine into two plastic tumblers, and handed them over to Susan. "I am going to turn off the lights now while I can still see a bit. There's no use to having the generator power something we won't need tonight."

She climbed back onto the air mattress and watched as Susan took a big swallow of the wine, her eyes closed. "OK, Gran, that was some first sip! But tell me what happened when you got to the motel. I guess I'll need to brace myself for the same thing tomorrow."

Susan took yet another swallow before continuing.

"If Chris hadn't been there to hold me, I know I would have fallen into the water and maybe passed out and drowned. I just collapsed in his arms. I mean, to me, it looked worse than anything I had ever seen."

Jo's eyes grew wide.

"There was sand up to the railings on all the buildings and the water was still pouring over from the ocean side onto the highway and over to the sound. Even with all the beach we had back then, the swell was huge and it just came on through. I could see places where shingles had been ripped off the roof and the front porch... well, I told you about that."

Susan's eyes seemed to be looking at the window but Jo

could tell she was seeing something completely different. A different time, long ago.

Susan shook her head. "That rocking chair was never seen again. I am sure it ended up in the sound. And the porch railing was just dangling. I started crying uncontrollably, and I remember Chris just holding me and telling me everything was fixable, everything would be OK."

Jo moved to be closer to her grandmother.

"We made it to the office and I realized as high as the water had come, it hadn't flooded there, so at least that was a positive. And then I just took a deep breath and started to figure out the next steps."

"With Chris?"

"Yes. With Chris," Susan said wistfully. "He was amazing. From that day on, I saw him every day. When he wasn't down at the harbor trying to sort through the mess there, he'd come by to see what I needed. He helped me get in touch with the guys who could help move the sand, and he worked with me to sweep what seemed like tons of sand off the porches." Susan closed her eyes before she continued. "All our help had evacuated at the last minute except for our maintenance man, Scott. But his house was really damaged by flood, so I didn't feel right asking him to spend time at the motel. And the road wasn't open for days, so it was only Chris and me."

"You said he was at the harbor too. What did he do there?"

"He was the mate on a boat. There was a captain named Terry Neal and he had a really nice boat and Chris worked his way up to become his mate. They had a great reputation for catching fish and having a good time and treating their customers right. But the boat was smashed to bits during the storm. Just about the whole fleet was gone."

Susan's eyes were tearing a bit, maybe remembering the devastation at the time and all those people who had seen their lives turned upside down.

"You can't imagine, Jo. Livelihoods gone just like that. Chris really worked hard to help out as much as he could. Just cleaning up was a massive chore. But he did that, and then he'd come and help me."

Jo couldn't help but think about Dare and the current fleet. Would things fare better this time around? She hoped so.

"What was the name of the boat, Gran?" Jo asked.

Susan took the final swig of the wine and looked at her granddaughter. As evenly as she could, she said, "The SeaAnna."

"Oh my God," said Jo. "That's crazy, Gran. Why would you do that? Name Mom after a boat? Does she know?"

A massive crack of thunder pierced the moment as if to add some divine punctuation to Jo's outburst. The house shook not only with the reverberation of the thunder but from a big gust of wind. The storm was getting into full swing now.

"Well, Jo," Susan seemed to be collecting her thoughts. "There's more to the story. You said you wanted to hear it, but I can stop now. You know enough even if you don't know it all."

Susan waited for Jo to say something, but she remained silent, so Susan went on. "Like I said, your mom never asked me any of this. When she was old enough to start asking, she just... didn't. She always acted like she didn't care to know." Susan's eyes were downcast. "And then she, well, she never gave me a chance. And it's been that way just about all her life."

Jo sat in the darkness but the lightning flashing made it

possible to see how strained her grandmother appeared. Should she learn the rest of the story? Would it make a difference? A million thoughts raced through her head about the past, the present, and the future. Maybe it would help if she knew. Maybe she could help mend fences. Maybe not, but it was worth a try.

"Yeah, Gran, I want to know as much as you want to tell me," Jo whispered. "I always figured it had to be something like this, but at least now I have a name."

"You have a face too even though you don't know it," Susan added. "Your mom and you both have a lot of Chris in you. Your smile especially and your mom's too, when she chooses to smile."

Jo instinctively touched her face. This man, this Chris, was a part of her, and a big part of her mom. It was hard to take in.

"So, where were we?" Susan seemed unsure of how to proceed. She took a deep breath and exhaled loudly. "OK. So, like I was saying, Chris and I spent all of our remaining time together in those weeks after the storm. And when we weren't working, we were on the beach."

Her voice had gone weaker, somehow with a faraway sort of tone. "Slowly, I got the motel back together. Your great-grandparents came down as soon as they could get onto the island but when they saw I had most everything under control, they went back to Richmond. Your grandfather's mom, Grandma Kent, was in a bad way and she needed them more than I did."

Jo was oblivious to everything except the sound of her grandmother's voice. The wind and thunder outside fading a bit as her focus was solely on Susan's story.

"It's amazing how people rally around here when there's a crisis. Debris got cleared up and piled up. Sand got moved. Roofs got fixed. And Chris and I fell in love. And it was on one of those nights that things came to their logical conclusion. You know what I mean."

Jo groaned inwardly. Maybe she had heard enough without too many details. But Susan seemed to sense that, and there was no need to say more on that subject.

"It was coming to the end of the season. We managed to piece together a Labor Day that was not bad business wise. A lot of people just wanted to come down to see what had happened." Susan had another glass of wine as if it would fortify her for what was coming. "Chris was mating on the few boats that could go out, and I was getting ready to go back to school. They had delayed the opening, as most of the coastal areas were hit, and that was enough of the student population to make a difference. Plus, some of the buildings on campus needed to be repaired. So, it was well into September before I needed to leave."

Jo realized she'd been holding her breath waiting for her grandmother to tell her what had happened.

"On our last night, although I didn't realize it, Chris and I were just counting shooting stars, when he mentioned how much he had loved the summer here, and how he was planning to try to stay a bit longer, maybe even permanently. He promised that he'd come by the next day and fix the last remaining bit of storm damage at the motel, the railing at the end of the porch." Susan sighed deeply and Jo noticed her voice started to quiver ever so slightly. "I was at the motel bright and early that morning, staying busy with odds and ends and trying to be sure things were in order for Scott who would manage the motel until my parents came back. They were trying to find a nursing home for Grandma Kent But by noon, when Chris still hadn't come, I decided to head down to the harbor and see what was up. It was always possible he'd had a last-minute charter. It happened some-times, and when it did he'd call me at the motel - but maybe he left too early for that."

Jo nodded slightly knowing that had happened with Dare a few times. But she was guessing that wasn't the case as she looked at her grandmother. Susan grimaced.

"When I got to the harbor, Chris was nowhere in sight. I asked around the docks but no one had seen him that day. Then I saw his roommate, Rob Wingate."

Susan heard Jo make a sharp intake of breath.

"Good grief, Gran. Rob Wingate? He's still around. Makes a nuisance of himself at the docks just about every day. No one sees him anywhere else, just there. Who knows what hole he lives in. He's a nasty piece of work, Dare says. Just trying to cause trouble."

"Yeah, well, he was the same then. I never had much to do with him, and as far as I knew, neither did Chris, they just roomed together. Rarely saw one another. Always had a cigarette hanging out of his mouth and smelled like tobacco and stale beer. Thought he was a real ladies' man."

Susan remembered that day as if it was yesterday. As she was talking, the memories were playing in her head as if she was living them.

When she approached Rob, she asked him where Chris was and he just kind of grinned.

"Didn't tell you, did he?" he sneered.

"Tell me what? she asked him.

"That he was leavin' today. Took off way before sunrise. Said he'd had enough of this hell hole and he was going' home, wherever that is."

Jo's mouth dropped open in disbelief, her anger rising, but by this time Susan had forgotten she was even there.

"Did he leave anything for me?" she asked in a rising panic.

"Hey," he shrugged. "That's the way it goes. You win some and you lose some. Think he had a girlfriend back home as well and she was probably after him to come on home. But since you're here, you need me for anything, Missy?"

"Hardly," she managed to choke out a reply.

"After that, heartbroken and lost, I pedaled faster than I ever had back to the motel and cried for the rest of the afternoon. Rest of the week, really. It didn't make sense to me, but, Jo, I wouldn't have been the first girl to be taken for a ride.

Susan hugged herself tightly and Jo came to her side to hug her as well.

"Back then, I had no way to catch up with him. We had no Facebook, no Google, and how was I going to find a Chris, Smith of all things, in the phone book of a town I didn't even know? Plus, the listing would be under his father's name, and the reality of it all suddenly hit me, and I remember just trying not to cry in front of Rob."

Jo started to say something but Susan shushed her.

"When my parents got back, I put it all behind me and focused on getting ready to go back to school. It wasn't until I was a few weeks in, doing a biology lab, when I got sick all over the place. Then it hit me." Susan turned away from Jo, not able to look her in the eyes. "For all my freedom and independence I thought I had, I'd forgotten to be responsible for myself. I was so head over heels with Chris that I felt certain there could be no consequences for our actions. But I was wrong. And once I told your great grandparents, that was it. They took me out of school, I came back to the island, and of course months later, your mom arrived."

Susan took a shaky breath, as if relieved she had arrived at the end of the story.

"I named her SeaAnna because that was a part of Chris, and when I called her name, I'd always have that connection to him."

Tears were streaming down Susan's face but Jo couldn't look. Her eyes were closed, listening to the relentless onslaught of the storm, finally knowing what her mom didn't want to know.

Her anger toward Chris burned inside her. He had deprived her of a grandfather and her mother of a father. But equally as important, her grandmother had been left alone and pregnant and devastated. If he had loved Susan, he would have gotten in touch. He'd have found a way. But all those years ago, he disappeared, to be a part of the mass of all the Chris Smiths who lived somewhere "up North," and he abandoned a family he didn't know he had.

She sensed movement and saw the silhouette of her grandmother getting up.

"Where are you going, Gran?"

"Just need to go to the bathroom, I can find my way in the dark, it's my house after all."

Then Jo heard a thud and a cry. She jumped up and flipped on the nearest light. The generator was clearly working. "Oh God, Gran, what happened?"

"I tripped on the edge of one of the throw rugs that usually isn't in my way, but we moved the couch. I've twisted my ankle," Susan groaned. "And I still need to get to the bathroom. Help me out, Jo. There's an old pair of crutches in the hall closet from when I had my knee surgery years ago."

Jo managed to find them and helped Susan navigate to the bathroom and back to the couch. "I'm getting some ice out of the fridge," she told her grandmother. "You'll need to keep it elevated for sure." Suddenly she stopped and remained silent for a second. "Listen, it's so quiet."

She and Susan listened. There was no sound of the wind or rain, and the whistling had disappeared. Looking out of the window, Jo could see a sliver of the moon and a few stars.

"Oh wow. We are in the eye. It's really something," Jo exclaimed.

"That it is, but, ouch, we need to get back into this fortress somehow before it cranks up again. There, I think I am settled."

Jo snuggled up next to her and gave her a hug. "Gran, I don't know what to say about all of that. It's a lot for me to process. I always knew there was someone, but I didn't know who or how or any of the circumstances. You've been so brave. But why is Mom so bitter?"

"I guess it's because she had such a tough childhood. When she was little, not one but both my parents became ill. I had to spend a lot of time taking care of them and trying to run the motel. When they died, I was devastated again and I retreated into my grief." Susan reflected for a moment.

"As for her, we might not have called it bullying then, but the kids made fun of her here on the island. While plenty of people got divorced here, at least the kids knew who both their parents were. She didn't and couldn't." She motioned for Jo to pour a little more wine in her glass.

"When SeaAnna was little, I didn't think it was right to tell her, and then later on, she just didn't want to hear it. It's like that was all a big black hole in her life. She couldn't wait to get away from here."

Jo had certainly heard from her mother on more than

one occasion how much she disliked the island. She motioned for Susan to go on.

"Well, once she went to college, that was it. She met Mike, they got married, and as you know, she only comes here if it's absolutely necessary. It's like if she didn't have a father to love, she wouldn't love me either. That I was somehow to blame." She shrugged. "I don't know, I'm not a psychologist. I just don't understand why the two of you have had it so rough. It's another source of sadness for me, but I am thankful you've not turned away."

"Oh Gran," Jo sobbed gently. "What a mess we have. But thank you for telling me. It's important."

The house heaved and both women grabbed for each other. "It's the backside," said Susan. "We are in for it now."

Chapter Three

It was the ringing of the phone that woke Jo. She struggled to get out from under all the pillows. Apparently, sometime during the night, Susan had crawled up onto the couch, where she was now with her injured foot propped up. It looked fairly swollen to Jo. The makeshift ice bag she'd made some hours before was nowhere in sight. She reached the phone after about five rings.

"Hello," she gasped, somewhat out of breath from her efforts.

"JoBell. Hearing your voice is a relief. OK. So, the landlines are working. How are you? How is your grandmother?"

"Dad. Hi," Jo was finally getting her bearings and was aware of the sun shining intermittently and of the fact that the deafening roar of the wind had diminished. She could see treetops still swaying and clouds racing, but she was not near enough to the windows to notice how much tide, if any, had reached their house. "We must have fallen asleep at some point. The storm was horrific last night and Gran took a fall. She's OK but she sprained her ankle. I tried to get ice on it but the ice melted and it's swollen. The generator is on, and I'm pretty sure I don't have cell service as that went out hours ago."

Jo realized she was shaking a bit.

"Dad, it was pretty scary but the house seems OK. I don't know about the motel yet. I'll go..."

"Jo," her Dad interrupted. "I can't imagine what it was like. From the reports we've seen and heard, the eye went right over you and there's a lot of flooding and structural damage. Of course, Highway twelve is closed. I hope you have enough supplies to get you through this until they get the road open. The storm is over land now and north of here. We got some wind and some rain but that's all. We were worried about you both but I knew that house would hold up."

Jo noticed his use of the word "we" and wondered why her mother didn't call. Then she heard SeaAnna's voice saying something in the background that Jo couldn't make out.

"What's Mom saying?" she asked.

"Oh, I've had you on speakerphone. She says she's glad you're OK and she hopes that sprain isn't too bad as there will be a lot of things that need to be done in these next days that would require your grandmother's attention," he said.

"Dad," said Jo not hiding her exasperation. "Gran will be OK and anything she needs to do she can do from here. I know they will work to have cell and internet back in a few days. And hey, I'm here and I've been working all summer. I do know a thing or two about this place. And I know Dare will be around to help me figure things out, assuming he has the time. If it's as bad as you say, I guess the harbor got waxed again."

"Waxed would be one way to put it from what I've heard. There's no video out from where you are, but just to the north and south it's pretty bad. Seems the storm churned up the coast so there's widespread damage. It's not catastrophic, but it's bad enough and it's going to mean a long clean up. I'm sure you and your grandmother are totally capable but, well, since your mom does own a portion of the motel, she feels she needs to...."

"Oh, I get it. It's mostly about the money part, the damage to her property. Not about me or Gran," Jo felt her voice shake a bit.

"Jo, don't. Just don't. Don't make this about the three of you. Of course, we care about you two, but thankfully, it sounds like you'll make it through these next few days. I think we'll plan to come once you see if the motel is habitable for the most part and of course we have to wait until they allow non-resident property owners access. I expect that to be days if not a week or so."

Jo looked up to see that Susan was now awake and listening with interest. Jo knew she could guess how the conversation was going.

"Tell your Dad of course it's fine if they come," Susan said as she attempted to maneuver into the crutches.

"Dad, I need to help Gran, so I'll call you later. I assume the landlines will keep working but you know they could go out too. I'll just try to keep in touch as much as I can. Don't worry. Thanks for calling."

Susan looked at Jo as she hung up the phone.

"Your Mom and Dad mean well, so of course they were going to try to get through if they could. Now my old-fashioned landline doesn't seem so silly, does it?" Susan asked.

"Hah. I guess not," admitted Jo. "And I'm glad they checked in, but why do they feel the need to come? Mom hates it here and Dad isn't crazy about it either. I never thought Mom cared much about the motel anyway, so why are they coming?"

She got the crutches under Susan's arms and helped her toward the bathroom.

Susan winced as she braced herself on the bathroom sink. "This ankle is hurting me more and more. Would you redo another bag of ice and then we'll take a look outside and see what we're dealing with? I haven't looked out yet and I don't think you have either."

Jo realized that between the phone call and helping Susan, she really hadn't looked outside at all other than that glimpse when she was talking to her father. She walked over to the window and looked out past the driveway. Just as Susan had remembered about Hurricane Evelyn, it seemed their house was like a floating bungalow in the Maldives. But instead of palm trees swaying, there were pieces of cedar and pine trees, limbs and branches, everywhere. Crab pots were bobbing along, and it looked like pieces of an oyster farm had found a new home against the fence rail next door. It was then Jo realized she could see the house next door which, for as long as she could remember, she hadn't been able to. The view to the neighbor Frank's home had been obscured by a beautiful live oak tree that now blocked the lane, its trunk split and gaping.

Susan came up behind Jo and placed her hand on her shoulder. "It's déjà vu for me, Jo," she sighed. "These storms just seemed to be carbon copies of one another. I can guess about the motel based on just the little bit I'm seeing, but we won't know until you lay eyes on it, and that won't be until this tide recedes a bit and we know there aren't any power lines down hiding in the water. I can't believe we both managed to fall asleep but I'm glad we did." Susan winced from the pain. "I wish I was still asleep because this ankle is really starting to throb."

"Let me move the couch back, and you're going to sit there as I get more ice and fix us some coffee. I really understand now why a generator is so important when you live down here." Shaking her head, her eyes were drawn out the window again. "I just can't believe what I'm seeing. How will we get that tree up?"

"Oh, I suspect Frank has a chain saw. And probably by later today it will be all in pieces," replied Susan. "You'll be amazed at how quickly things bounce back. There will be plenty of devastation, to be sure. But people here are truly resilient and we pull together in times like this. I know that as soon as the road opens, the charities will come on in, like the Red Cross and such, but our own CERT people will already have started to get aid organized and will be providing all the assistance and support they can."

"CERT?" asked Jo.

"Community Emergency Response Team," said Susan. "They are folks who live right here and are prepared to mobilize right away and do what they can. I wouldn't be surprised if they aren't already communicating and figuring out where to set up and what's needed most. They really are amazing." Susan looked at Jo. "You know, Dare's mom is involved in that, I think."

She was interrupted by the landline ringing again. Jo picked it up, mouthed "Dare" to Susan, and smiled.

"Oh, hey Dare," she said. "We were just talking about your mom. Isn't she part of CERT? Gran thinks she is."

"Yes, she is, but I'd like to know how you two are doing. Glad Mom and Dad kept this landline. Mom always says it's for emergencies when I tease her, and I guess she's right. Did y'all come through this blow OK?"

"I think so," Jo responded. "The house shook like crazy but we didn't have any broken windows or anything. There's tide here with stuff floating all around and a big live oak tree, the one next door, came down and is blocking the lane between this house and Frank's. Of course, we have the generator but cable went out hours ago and the internet too. No cell, but you know that. What are you hearing or seeing? I'm guessing you're all OK too?"

"We are. But it's a mess here. I don't even want to think about the harbor and all the boats and whatnot strewn all over the place. Mom's been on the phone with CERT folks and it seems like it's water everywhere, so there will be lots of flood damage. Apparently, it's real bad by the school and the highway was breached up north in several places. I guess the electric co-op will try to get out as soon as the wind diminishes. That will be the first priority – power. But you both made it safe and sound, then? That's great news."

"Well," Jo hesitated. "Gran twisted her ankle pretty good last night. She fell over a rug. I've got it elevated and put some ice on it. Any other suggestions?"

"Give her some Tylenol or whatever she wants for pain, I guess," said Dare. "I know that's what we do down at the docks when someone falls. With all the ropes and stuff lying around you'd be surprised at how often that happens. Visitors mostly. They are looking at everything and not paying attention. A swollen ankle can sure ruin a vacation."

"Speaking of visitors," said Jo. "I guess it will be quite a while before we have some. I had hoped to end up this summer on a high note, but this isn't the note I was looking for."

"Cheer up," Dare said. "I know it's bad. And it's going to be a mess for a while. But you'll be amazed at how quickly things get back to some semblance of normal."

"That's what Gran just said. The resilience of the islanders or something like that."

"Well, she's right," he said. "And in fact, as soon as I can manage to get Dad's truck onto the road and Mom gives me the OK about any downed power lines, I'll come and pick you up and we'll check out the motel. I'm guessing Gran will stay put."

"Yes, she will," she said. "Let me know when you're coming and I'll walk down the lane out to the edge of the highway. There's too much debris and stuff to bring the truck back here. And if there's still a lot of tide, don't worry about getting me. I'll just get out there as soon as I can. Guess we're all in the same boat more or less."

She hung up the phone.

"So nice of him to call, wasn't it?" asked her grandmother.

"Yes, Dare's such a good friend." Then she turned and headed out of the living room.

"Well, guess I'll fix us some breakfast. Not much else to do but watch the tide go down and the crab pots roll by. Let me get you that Tylenol."

It was later in the afternoon before Dare phoned to say

39

he'd be by, but it would be slow going. Jo put on her boots and stuffed her work gloves into her jeans.

"Gran, I'll take some photos with the phone for you. Don't worry about us. You know we'll be careful. Just make sure you stay put," Jo advised.

"I am not going anywhere, for sure," replied Susan. "This foot is more swollen than I thought it would be. I think I'll start making a list of the things I'm pretty sure we'll need to follow up on. That's a start. But I won't move from this couch."

Jo nodded as she waved, blew her a kiss, and closed the door behind her. The wind was gradually dropping and while it was breezy, it wasn't any more gusty than most Hatteras days. The sun had broken through the clouds enough to make it plenty warm outside, and she thought of how the mosquitoes would be having a field day in the next week. When she got to the bottom of the steps, she moved into the water carefully. It was about mid-calf but she could see from the marks on the house pilings it had been higher than that during the height of the storm. Then the water level would have been up over her knees.

She made it out to the highway by keeping to the center of the lane and steering clear of anything suspicious floating around. She turned back to look at the roof of Gran's house, and saw perhaps where a shingle or two was missing but, remarkably, nothing more. She had only been standing at the end of the lane for a minute or two when Dare appeared in his dad's old Ford.

She hopped in and asked, "Doesn't he care about all the salt water and what it'll do to this truck?"

"He says it's so old now he'd be glad if the salt got to it. But he always hoses it off and he keeps it running somehow. It's good for times like these. Really glad we got your gran's car to the airport. The tide ran high but it wouldn't have gotten that high for sure. Or we wouldn't be here."

Dare drove slowly so as not to make a wake. A few other vehicles were starting to move along the highway - sheriff's vehicles, Park Service trucks, power company trucks, and some of the locals interested in checking out the surf at the motels or taking a few photos and videos to post as soon as the internet returned. It seemed to Jo that everything was moving in slow motion. She felt shock and fear in the pit of her stomach, but at the same time it was incredible to see the power of nature. Dare slowed even further and then turned into the parking lot of the Salty Seas restaurant. "I'm afraid it's got to be on foot from here, Jo. I've heard through Mom the water is still pouring across the highway from the oceanfront. Don't want to push this truck to its demise any sooner than necessary."

They walked silently, listening to the sounds of the island trying to reawaken as if from a bad dream. The sound of chainsaws mixed with the cry of the gulls, and the ocean roared with a swell that was still powerful. Foam was flying around them and the smell of the saltwater and seaweed was overpowering. Crab pots, pieces of what had been sand fences, and unidentifiable trash floated along beside them and they had to be careful not to step on nails, if they could see them.

When they reached the edge of the motel property Jo tried to take it all in without panic. There was sand up to the porch decks, so that meant five feet of sand covering their two parking lots. She realized that was tons of sand. Bare places on the roof were testimony to the fury of the winds the motel experienced. They weren't able to walk around to the oceanfront as the waves were still breaking under the buildings, but she expected that at least some of the porch railings would need to be repaired. And there was no way to know if sand and water had gotten into the lower floor guest rooms. Even though they too were on pilings above the beach level, the wind could push the sand right under the doors and through every little crack. Broken windows meant the rain could have gotten inside. The alarm for the septic system was blaring incessantly but at the moment there was nothing they could do to stop it. A cable line had been disconnected from the power pole and danced wildly in the air. Jo tried to process everything but it all became a blur in her mind. She wanted to have a plan, she wanted to know how to proceed, but all she felt was overwhelmingly sad and helpless. She hated when she didn't feel in control.

"I... I don't know what to think," Jo stammered. "How will we ever get this all back together again? Gran is going to be beside herself."

"She'll probably take it in stride," Dare mused. "She's used to storms and nor'easters and such. This one is bad, but the buildings didn't float away, and believe it or not, she probably has sand removal guys on her speed dial on that old landline." His hand was on her shoulder, giving her strength. Support. "I know it looks overwhelming, but trust me, from what I saw driving up here, you, Gran, my folks, and this motel are going to be OK." Dare shook his head trying to be both reassuring but honest. "I've seen enough damage to know we'll be limping along for a while getting everyone back together. It's the roofing damage you need to be most concerned about."

"Who's going to do that?" Jo wondered aloud. "Getting stuff fixed around here is a nightmare even in normal times."

"Oh, you wait, there'll be people coming in as soon as

the County gives the OK. Repair people of all kinds. Some
are decent and some are rip-offs. But for sure we'll need to
use their services, the good ones, that is. Social media weeds
out the bad ones pretty quickly. You'll wanna keep up with
the locals' pages on Facebook." Dare took Jo by the shoulders. "I'm not going to lie to you. We're all in for a challenge. But most of the folks who come in on the early
admission for work really want to help out." Jo looked skep-
tical, but Dare continued. "Yeah, they'll make money but
they do good work. Word travels on the island grapevine
about the ones who are here just to take advantage of the
situation. You'll figure it out." He looked at her seriously.
"Just keep your eyes and ears open."

Jo mulled over all that she'd be doing in the next days
and weeks before she headed back to campus. She
wondered if there would be a delay, that thought hadn't
occurred to her. Her dad said damage all up and down the
coast. That probably included the campus in Wilmington.

"Boy, it's a lot, Dare." She looked at him. "But that's not
all. My parents are coming down as soon as they'll allow
non-resident property owners onto the island. You know
how I feel about that. I guess when it rains, it pours."

Dare glanced over and wondered if she realized the
pun. But he also knew Jo and her parents had a tangled relationship. He felt for her. He reached over and gave her a
hug. They watched a few more waves roll across the
highway and then turned back to walk toward the truck.

Chapter Four

The days after the storm seemed to be as much of a whirlwind as the days of preparation ahead of it. It amazed Jo to see how quickly things seemed to bounce back, as bad as they were. Her grandmother had seen to it that the sand removal crew she always used was on the spot the day the tides stopped overwashing the parking lot. They moved literally tons of sand to the oceanfront and the soundside where it looked as though a new dune had been created. The wind was already softening some of that landscape, and the sun had dried up the water that lay in puddles not only in the motel lot, but also in most of the low spots all over the island.

The water that remained was bringing the mosquitoes, but even that problem wasn't as bad as she had expected.

The power had been restored in two days, and again, Jo reflected on how wise Gran had been to install the generator a few years back. At least in the evenings when she went back home after a long day, she had cool air to greet her along with supportive smiles and questioning from Susan. Her foot was still a bit puffy and sore, and Jo insisted she not navigate the steep steps up and down to the house for a few more days. Surprisingly, Susan agreed. She had done all of the insurance work by phone or email, and seemed content to read and relax, and let Jo tell her what was happening with the clean-up.

The main issue now was getting visitors back on the island. Contractors were being allowed on as of today, she'd heard, along with any residents who had evacuated. Tomorrow non-resident property owners would be allowed. That meant visitors would be coming back shortly after that. SeaAnna had texted to let her know they'd be arriving around midday tomorrow and she'd hoped Jo would have a room ready. Her dad had also texted to say not to worry, that everything would be fine and they were looking forward to seeing her and Susan, and how was Susan by the way?

The two texts were a wonderful example of the ping-pong ball kind of relationship Jo had had with her parents for as long as she remembered. Her mom would be short, cold, and always very much to the point. Her dad was the one who would be there to soften the hard edges and remind her she was very much loved by both of them, even if it wasn't always evident. She was sitting on the motel porch, taking a quick break from answering phones for people who were clamoring to get back to the island. She got lost in thought trying to think about how she might improve things with SeaAnna, and if she really wanted to, when she was interrupted by a text from Dare.

"What time r u off? Let's go by Marcie's for a drink. "

"I think I can manage 6. K?" she texted back.

"K CU"

She texted back a "thumbs up" emoji and went back inside to be sure everything was as it should be. Having the housekeepers clean the rooms before the storm was at her gran's insistence and Jo would be forever grateful. Very little had to be done to get ready for her parents, or indeed anyone who wanted to stay at the motel. The big remaining issue was the roof, but the problems there did not preclude people from staying, at least in the short run. She'd have to talk to Gran about finding a roofer now that contractors were on the island.

She fielded a few more calls, checked in with her maintenance crew, and locked up behind her. Marcie's Bar and Grille was just a mile or so away. Locally owned, it had always been the meeting place for locals, and once Marcie reopened after the storm, it was even more so. Everyone needed a place to just relax and try to unwind. Relief and recovery efforts were discussed and, in true island fashion, the latest news and gossip was always exchanged.

Jo walked in and Dare was already waiting at the end of the bar at their usual spaces.

"God, I am wiped out," said Jo as she plopped onto the seat next to him. "It's going well for us, but I just worry about everyone else. I guess I feel guilty we didn't fare as badly as some people. We're pretty much ready to open."

"Be careful what you wish for, honey," said Marcie as

she placed the usual glass of lemonade in front of Jo. "A lot of people don't want tourists back so quickly. Lots of gawkin' and all. It's a fine line between doin' business and openin' up the island to folks who don't understand what we've been through."

"Hmm," Jo said. "I hadn't thought of it that way. I'm sure Gran has thoughts on that."

"I'm sure she does. How's her ankle?" asked Marcie, as she wiped the sweat from her brow. "It's been really busy today what with the contractors coming on the island and all. I miss seeing Susan."

"She's coming along," Jo replied turning to Dare. "Hey you, sorry I haven't even said hello. Have you ordered?"

Dare asked Marcie to bring him a Wild Whelk, one of the local beers. "You know," he turned to Jo. "Marcie would probably give you a beer if you asked."

"Yeah, I know. But she and Gran go back for forever, and if I did anything to screw up her license, Gran would never forgive me, and neither would anyone on this island. Gran lets me drink wine at the house, so I can really go crazy there. And for sure I'll need a glass or two or three tonight. You remember my parents are coming tomorrow."

Dare took a swig of beer. "You know, I have tried really hard since I was old enough to think about these things, to figure out why you and your mom are so distant with each other. How far back does all this go?"

Jo looked at Dare carefully. "You and I have been friends for so long, I guess I just never talk about it much. I don't even know if I understand it all. But I think I messed up her life somehow and she's never figured out how to deal with that other than to resent me."

"Messed up her life? How? You're her daughter, like the

only child, and you're smart and hard-working and, you know, pretty damn cool. What's to mess up?" Dare asked.

"One time, when I was a teenager, like thirteen, I think, we had a big argument," Jo began. Then she paused and took a breath. "I was home from boarding school. You knew I was sent away to school, right? From first grade. Rarely saw my parents during the school year and then you know I was here for a month in the summers with Gran. On either side of that month were camps and stuff like that. Mom and me, I don't know, we just didn't really know one another. I couldn't understand how the other girls at school talked about their moms so much and how great they were and the things they did together. Dad tried to make up for it, but he's my dad, not my mom. Anyway, we were really shouting at each other and she said..." she let her voice fade to silence. Shaking her head. "Doesn't really matter right now, but I just couldn't ever forget what she said. And I still haven't. It hurts like hell, but I just put up a wall. We're civil to one another for the most part. And Dad still tries to mediate."

She stopped and Dare brushed a tear from her face.

"Whoa, that's a lot. I'm sorry. I don't know what to say. But I mean, she just said one thing one time and your whole relationship got fucked up due to that? Can't you try to make it better? My mom and sister fight all the time but they get over it. Maybe if you –"

Jo cut him off. "Dare, don't go there. This is my thing with my mom. Your fantastic family with perfect grandparents, two for each parent, and you and your sister have it made. I can't compete with your perfection, so don't tell me what to do."

Dare sat back a little stunned. "OK. I'm gonna just forget you said all that because I'm not sure where it came from. I get it that you're tired, really tired, and that your parents are coming and you're pretty anxious about that. So, let's try this. I was going to ask you if you wanted to go down to the docks to hear Jamie and the Hanks in a bit. They're playing a Hurricane Eva relief mini-concert for the locals."

"You know, Dare, I just don't feel like it. Why don't you go yourself? I wouldn't be good company."

"Suit yourself," he said getting up from the bar. "If I thought there was something in that lemonade, I'd give you a pass on what you just said, but since it's just lemonade and you didn't say you were sorry, I guess I will go. Sorry I asked."

"Just go, Dare," Jo responded wearily. "Just go ahead and go."

Dare dropped some cash next to her. "This is for my beer, your lemonade, and leave Marcie a nice tip. Have a good evening."

Jo didn't acknowledge him. She looked away until she saw him walking across the parking lot. Then she shed another tear, turned her back to the doorway, and sat staring at the glass of lemonade.

Chapter Five

Jo sat for a long time deep in thought. Why had she lashed out at Dare like that? He'd never been anything but understanding and kind to her. She never realized how much she envied him for what she saw as a "normal" family arrangement. He had wonderful parents, doting grandparents on both sides – Jo had met them on many occasions during the summers when they would visit the island – and he had a younger sister who was as sweet and kind as she was determined and smart. But none of that was because of Dare's doing. She knew she was wrong for allowing her anger and hurt to color their friendship by trying to hurt him. She shook her head and decided she would text him first thing early in the morning to apologize. Then her heart skipped as she realized he might not accept it. But deep down inside she knew while she might be crazy emotional at times, Dare was rock steady. He was truly a special guy.

"Excuse me, but is this seat taken?" asked a deep voice and Jo looked up to see someone who, in a brief instant, looked vaguely familiar to her. She realized he was speaking to her because she'd set her backpack on the adjacent bar stool after Dare left, hoping to be alone in her thoughts. Clearly, the bar was slammed as every other seat was occupied, and the servers, MaryAnn and Carolyn, had all they could handle with the tables, so there wasn't much she could do but move the pack.

"No, please, it's OK," she shrugged.

"Hey, if you're waiting for someone, I can go sit outside or something," he said. "Looks like everything in here is taken."

"Nah, I was just being a little selfish putting my bag there. Have a seat," Jo replied.

Marcie came over and asked him for his order. "What'll it be Mr. new to my bar?"

"Name is Jonathan. I'll take a burger and fries, please. And whatever the local brew is these days," he said.

"That would be a 'Wild Whelk'," she replied, and the man broke into a big smile.

"Well, that's a new one on me," he chuckled.

Again, Jo had the strangest feeling she should know him, but he clearly came in alone with none of the locals. So maybe he was one of the contractors who came in today. He seemed at ease, though, like he knew his way around.

"Hey Jo, come back to earth." It was Marcie again. "Do you want another lemonade?"

"Yeah, 'cause I'm gonna order food for me and Gran to take home. I'm too tired to cook tonight and I know she loves your fried shrimp basket. And I'll have a burger like my next-door neighbor here."

"You got it," said Marcie and she hustled back to the kitchen with the orders, and then went for their drinks.

She looked over and gave the man a smile. "I'm guessing you're a contractor, since it's only been locals since Eva paid us a visit."

"You're pretty sharp," he replied. "Yep, that's my van out there. JCS Roofing. From just outside of Baltimore. My crew came down too, in another truck. We're hoping to help out."

Jo turned and looked back out through the doorway where she could just make out some of the lettering on a burgundy van.

"That's really nice of you, assuming you're legit," Jo said.

He looked at her to see if she was joking but there was no trace of the smile he'd seen earlier.

"I see you're serious. I know a lot of scammers come after storms but you don't need to put that label on me, and I'd appreciate it if anyone else says anything like that to you, you set them straight. I came with letters of reference and anyone can look at our social media pages to see what kind of business we are."

Jo relaxed a bit. How lucky could she be to have a legitimate roofer appear magically next to her just when she was beginning to wonder how she and Gran would find someone.

"Well, that's good to know because I definitely need a

roofer," she said.

"Your house lose some shingles?" he asked.

"Not my house, my motel. And it's more than just some shingles, it's a whole lot of shingles and probably some things I can't even see or describe."

"You own a motel?" He raised his eyebrows and set his beer down, looking at her with interest.

"Oh, I didn't mean I own it. I manage it. Well, I do in the summers. Truthfully, actually this is my first summer. But I know it really well. I've been coming here since I was a kid. My gran owns it. But she's kind of laid up now with a hurt ankle from the night of the storm, so I'm trying to take care of things so she doesn't have to worry much. I think this storm took something out of her. Reminded her a lot of a bad storm years ago. I'd prefer she not see the place until we've got it all together again. The sand has been removed and all the other issues have been taken care of. Except the roof."

"Well, I'd be glad to have my crew take a quick look at it. Which motel is it?" He asked.

"It's the Hatteras Hideaway, it's the first one you come to..."

"Oh, I know it very well, "he interrupted. "I helped put that place back together once before."

"You did? That motel has been in my family for forever so you must have done some work for someone I know!" she exclaimed.

"Well, I don't know about that. This was ago, nineteen seventy-five, when Evelyn came through. I was working here for the summer on a boat, but after the storm, I tried to help out property owners where I could since the boats were pretty much all gone. At least the one I mated for," he said.

"But in seventy-five my great-grandparents owned the motel. They were the Kents. You had to know them," Jo said.

"Kent?" Jonathan's demeanor suddenly changed. "I never knew them, but I knew of them. Their daughter was managing the motel that summer just like you are now. Her name was Susan. Susan Kent. Hmmmm. Imagine that. And you say she still owns that motel? I'm not sure she'd welcome me back to help this time around."

He put his burger on the plate, half eaten and placed two twenties on the bar as he got up to leave.

"Wait a minute," Jo said. "Why would you say that? My gran is one of the most well-respected people on this island and she treats everyone pretty fairly as far as I know."

"Well, a nice way to put it is that we didn't end things on the best of terms," he replied.

The wheels in Jo's brain were moving so quickly she couldn't quite process everything she was thinking. "What do you mean, end things?"

"Look," he said. "I never expected to be having this conversation. I knew your grandmother, Susan, very well. But that was a long time ago and that's water over the dam. I'm sure she's never given a second thought to what happened to old Chris."

"But you are Jonathan. I heard you, and you said your company was JCS Roofing," Jo stammered. Her heart was racing and her throat was suddenly dry. She reached for her lemonade.

"I did and it is," he said looking at her carefully. "JCS. Jonathan Christopher Smith. But back in the day everyone knew me as Chris and...."

Jo started to say something but nothing would come out. That's when she fainted.

"Good God," he called out. "I need some help over here."

Marcie flew from behind the bar counter and yelled, "Carolyn, get the door. Let's get her outside to get some air. Looks like she fainted."

Chris and Marcie together managed to get her outside and under a tree. "MaryAnn, grab some water," Marcie yelled. Then she looked at Chris carefully. "Did you say something to her? What did you do?"

Chris stood up and looked Marcie in the eye. "I have no idea what happened. We were talking about a roofing job and then I realized I knew her family and then she passed out. She seemed really agitated but I swear I didn't say or do...."

Mary Ann brought the water and lifted Jo up to a sitting position just as her eyes started to flutter. "Whhhaaa...What happened? I ..." she said, almost in a whisper. Then her eyes fell on Chris. "You. You bastard," she shouted.

Chris threw his hands up in the air. "I don't know what the hell is going on here but I think you need some rest or something stronger than that lemonade you're drinking. And I can assure you I won't be doing your roofing job. Find someone else."

He looked at Marcie and said, "I think you need to find some help for this young lady. I left enough money to cover my bill on the counter. Sorry for the disturbance. I'm leaving."

"Oh no," said Jo more calmly, but there was a dark look on her face. "You'll wait to hear what I have to say to you. Marcie, you go on inside. MaryAnn and Carolyn, you too. I'm OK. Just tired, I guess. I'll be fine. But this guy and I have some unfinished business. He doesn't know it but I do, and he's going to hear me out."

The three women walked back to the restaurant door, but Marcie turned around and mouthed to Jo, "Scream if you need me."

Chris kept walking toward his truck but Jo went after him, a bit unsteady but determined. He was opening his door when Jo grabbed his arm and looked him straight in the eye. "Why did you leave my gran the way you did? She was pregnant. But you never knew that because you left. And you know what? She had a baby girl. My mom. And then my mom had me. And I guess you can figure out what that means."

Jo was nearly choking with the sobs that were overtaking her. "It means, Mr. Jonathan Christopher Smith, you're my grandfather."

Chris stopped for a moment and then took a deep breath and exhaled.

"That's some story, young lady. I don't know your name but let me just say this. Susan Kent, your grandmother, could have called me. It might have been long distance but she could have reached out to me. Given what we'd shared and then what I had to deal with, it was the very least I expected. Even if it was just to say good-bye. But she didn't. OK? And that hurt. A lot. So, now you know."

"Wait, "Jo said with a look of confusion on her face. "My gran, Susan, never knew how to get in touch with you. You left with no phone number, no address. How was she going to find you in nineteen seventy-five with no information?"

"Oh, I left information all right. That night I got a call that my father had a massive heart attack. It was really the middle of the night and so I left a detailed note with my roommate Rob something or another. He promised me he'd get it to Susan. I left the island and drove straight through until I got home. My dad died about a week later. My mom was an absolute wreck. I kept thinking I'd get a call from Susan but I never did. I ended up having to step in and take over the business. It wasn't six months later, my mom died. She just couldn't live without him. I had my hands full and a million things to think about and deal with. But Susan never called and you know, life went on."

"Rob Wingate," Jo said.

"Yeah, that's right. How do you know him? My God, is he still alive? I thought he'd be dead from drink or drugs or both," Chris asked.

"Well, for one thing, he's still around and he's a nasty piece of work," Jo replied. "For another, my gran, your Susan went down to the docks the day you didn't show up and asked around. She specifically asked Rob, of course. And you know what? He said you'd left in the middle of the night because you'd had enough and, more importantly, that you had a girl back home who'd been pestering you to return. So no, he didn't give her the note."

Chris rocked back on his heels and they were both quiet for a moment. Then Chris spoke. "But that doesn't necessarily make me your grandfather. I mean, who did Susan marry? How many kids did she have? You're trying to make something fit that doesn't fit."

"I'm pretty sure it does all fit," said Jo. "You see, Gran never married. She went back to school a few weeks after you disappeared. Then about three weeks after that she got sick in biology lab and realized she was pregnant. My great-grandparents were not thrilled. They yanked her out of school and told her she could help them with the motel. Mom was born and then, before she turned two, both of Susan's parents got sick and she had to care for them, and a baby, for years. My great-grandparents both passed away

57

when Mom was about five or six and by then she was so immersed in running the motel that she inherited, she just kept on. Never had any interest in anyone else. Just put all her time and energy into raising SeaAnna."

Chris's shoulders sagged just a bit and there was a sharp intake of breath. "She named her SeaAnna?"

"Yeah – isn't that the boat you mated on for Captain Neal?" Jo queried.

"It was." Chris exhaled. "And you are?

"I'm Jo. Jo Leonard. Short for JoBell. Don't know why I was named that, but according to my mom, my gran really asked her to do it."

"I used to pick JoBells for Susan and put them in little dishes of water," Chris sighed. "Look, I'm having a hard time getting my head around what you're saying. It's a lot."

"Yeah, no joke," said Jo. "And you don't know the half of it. Your daughter and I have never been on the best of terms and Gran thinks you dumped her. What do I say to them? And what am I supposed to think about you? How am I supposed to feel? My whole life I wanted a husband for Gran, a father for Mom, and a grandfather for me like everyone else. But now I'm just confused. And I'm not sure if I believe you."

She stopped and took in the immensity of what had happened over the last hour or so. Now she knew why he had looked familiar to her. Her mother had the same sandy hair now tinged with gray and there was no mistaking the smile. It was her smile too, she'd been told. Now she knew where it came from.

They both just stared at each other. "Well, I could say the same thing, at least about not knowing how to feel. I never married either. Just didn't have time. Taking care of the business was a huge responsibility. It still is. Family just didn't seem to be in the cards. And maybe I don't believe you either. But I know one way to figure this out in addition to DNA testing. Will you please text your number to me at the cell number on the van? I'll be in touch."

Jo surprised herself and said, "Please text me or call me. We have to figure this out and I don't want you to disappear again."

Chris got into the van as Jo texted her number to him. She heard his phone ping. "Got it," he said. "Look, JoBell Leonard, I am not the person your grandmother has made me out to be. And maybe she's not the person I thought she was all these years. I have to figure this all out. But I will be back in touch."

She watched him drive out of the parking lot, and noticed a few sideways glances as she walked back into the restaurant.

"Hey girl, do you want to tell me what that was all about?" asked Marcie. "By the way, I redid your order as it got ice cold. Susan wouldn't go for that."

"Thanks for that. Um, I'm not really into sharing at the moment, Marcie. Sorry. It's, well, it's personal," Jo replied, as she handed Marcie the money for the order.

"Well, I hope that fellow is OK. I mean, you know, he's old enough to be your grandfather," Marcie said. Jo turned white and her mouth went completely dry as the truth of Marcie's statement hit home. "You know, Jo, you look like you've seen a ghost. Fainting isn't good. I think you'd better get on home, eat, and get some sleep."

Jo nodded wearily, suddenly so tired it hurt to even think. "You don't know the half of it, Marcie," she said as she walked out the door. And then, as she looked up at the sky, she thought, "You're closer to the truth than you know."

Chapter Six

Jo wearily climbed the steps to the house. She was so tired and yet there was this surge of energy running through her. Had she really met her grandfather? Everything seemed to point in that direction. But what if Gran hadn't been entirely truthful with her. Maybe there had been someone else? It was the seventies after all, and wasn't that the generation of sexual liberation and free love? Perhaps she didn't want Jo to know she'd been "loose" as the term was back in the day. But not Gran. Gran already had shared so much, why hold that back? That wouldn't make sense.

"Jo, honey, is that you?" Gran called from the back of the house. "I kind of expected you a bit earlier. It's late to be cooking dinner."

Jo managed to gather herself and answered, "No worries. I was at Marcie's for a while longer than I expected so I brought you some take out."

"Fried shrimp basket," Susan said as she hobbled into the kitchen. "And before you throw a hissy at me, I am tired of those crutches and I can manage fine. In a day or two, I'll be ready to get back to business."

Jo smiled. She loved Susan's tenacity and her positive attitude. She was one strong woman. "Here's your shrimp basket, Gran. And Marcie says to say hey and she's hoping to see you soon."

"Marcie is a gem, for sure," said Susan. She delved into the shrimp and fries with gusto and then looked up at Jo. "You look a bit peeked. Are you alright? I'm thinking you are really pushing it at the motel getting ready for your mom and dad tomorrow and you've got yourself all worked up. Am I right?"

"Probably," Jo replied, thankful that Susan had given her a ready-made excuse. "But things really do look good. I think they'll be pretty happy with how quickly we've put things back together. The sand piles look a little rough but they'll smooth over with time. Just the roof now...." Her voice trailed off.

"A few folks have been checking in on me and I heard that a whole slew of contractors came onto the island today. I'm sure we'll find someone. They are here looking for business and we can give them that. Just have to be sure they aren't crooked."

Jo pretended to be deeply involved in enjoying her burger. She hoped she could excuse herself and head for bed. She needed to think. Her head throbbed.

"You said you were at Marcie's a little later than you expected," asked Susan. "Everything OK there?"

"Sure," replied Jo trying to think of how to make up the best little white lie. "Um, Dare was there and he and I got into a little spat. Took us a while to work through it but it's all good now."

"Glad to hear it," said Susan. She appeared to be satisfied and let the subject drop. But then she was on to another sensitive topic.

"About your mom and dad coming," she began. "You know, Jo, I have always struggled with why your mom and I don't have the best relationship but I do understand it. I keep hoping over time it will get better but a lot of time has passed. I still keep hoping. You never lose hope with your child. But I also hope that the two of you can become closer."

"Gran," Jo interjected, "I'm so tired and really don't think I want to go down that road again right now."

"Just hear me out," Susan said. "You had a wonderful education, even though boarding school wasn't your thing and it did keep you apart from your folks. But your parents have both only wanted the best for you. I know neither one of them particularly cares for the island but they allowed you to come and stay with me for years. You saw it as them wanting to 'get rid' of you for a month each summer. But I think, in fact I know, they saw how you flourished here and how much you loved everything about this place. I suspect your mom sees a lot of me in you and sometimes that's hard for a parent to accept. Genetics are a funny thing and sometimes traits and interests and talents skip right through one generation onto the next. Now, your dad wasn't raised here, so I'm not surprised he isn't a coastal person. Some people just don't like the sea and the sand and all. Your mom was raised here but she has too many bad memories. You, however, were drawn here like a magnet. And you love studying jellyfish as much as I did. I love seeing you follow in my footsteps. You'll do the research I never could complete and that's a great thing. But it wouldn't have happened if you hadn't spent so much time here."

"But, Gran," Jo pleaded. "Mom hurt me. Not with actions, she never beat me or anything, but her words hurt more than I could handle. I never told you that, but she did. Once. A long time ago. She tried to take it back but I can't forget it."

"And how long ago was this?" Susan asked.

"I was twelve or thirteen, I think. We were having an argument about something stupid. I probably told her I hated her or something but I didn't really mean I hated her. I was just so mad."

"Ha. There you go, Jo," Susan said. "You told her you hated her but you didn't mean it, and yet, you are certain that she meant whatever it was she said that hurt you. Does that really make sense to you? And you're telling me you hardened your heart to her for all these years because of that?" Gran shook her head. "JoBell, I am more than a bit surprised. Life is too short. She is your mom. Her experience was not the same as yours. She was always absent one parent but you have two. And to be honest, I think your dad is really getting tired of trying to be the go-between with the two of you. Think about all of this tonight and see if you can't try to at least start to mend fences when she gets here tomorrow. Someone has to make the first step. Will you try?"

Jo looked at her grandmother with her eyes full of tears,

but not for the reasons Susan thought. "I will try, Gran," she said. "But it still hurts."

"Hurts only hurt as long as you let them," replied Susan. "Now I will do a bit of clean up here in this kitchen, not that there's much. Take a shower and get to bed."

Jo was grateful for the reprieve. She stripped down and stepped into the hot shower and let the water run over her, mixing with her tears. It was all too much to take in at once. It shamed her to admit that she had let the wound of her mother's comments fester over the years, and that maybe it was time to let it go and try to let it heal. She stayed in the shower for as long as she felt she reasonably could without wasting too much water and causing any suspicion with Gran. Then she headed for bed.

She started to think about herself, SeaAnna, Dare, Susan, and of course, Chris. But she didn't get anything settled because within a few minutes she was sound asleep.

When the light started to come into her window at dawn the next morning, Jo felt anything but refreshed. She had had too many strange dreams with her mother, grand-mother, possible grandfather, and Dare all jumbled together. She couldn't remember details, just that the dreams were unsettling.

But she remembered the promise she made to herself at Marcie's the night before, before Chris had entered the picture, and so she reached for her phone and texted Dare.

U up? Need to talk. And apologize. Sorry. Can we walk and talk?

She had to wait less than a minute before Dare responded.

That was rough. But OK. Accepted. I need to talk to you too. Meet at motel at 7?

K she typed.

She looked at the clock. 6:30. Just enough time. She threw on some shorts and a T-shirt and scribbled a note for Susan. She grabbed a yogurt from the fridge. Just as she was about to leave, her grandmother called out to her, "Jo, is that you leaving already? Everything OK?"

"Yes, Gran," she said. "Just meeting Dare for an early morning walk. I'll be back before I head to the office. Sleep in, OK?"

Susan appeared at her bedroom door. "Jo, you know I can't sleep in. Never could. But I'll have some real breakfast for you, so don't be too long. Office should be open by eight-thirty as you know."

"I know, I know," Jo called out from down the steps. Yogurt did not qualify as breakfast to Susan. "I'll be back in plenty of time. Gotta run now."

When Jo got to the motel, Dare was already waiting at the top of the small barrier dune, much smaller now since Eva, his silhouette recognizable with the sun coming up behind him.

"God, Dare, I have so much to tell you," Jo panted, setting her bike under the building.

"I think I broke a record getting here. Gran wants me to be sure to have the office open at eight-thirty if not sooner."

"And I have a story for you," said Dare. "So, who's first?"

They started walking down to the water's edge and turned right, the rising sun to their backs just a bit, and a nice breeze from the southeast. The water was a beautiful sea greenish blue color and perfectly clear.

"You go," said Jo. "Because I'll need lots of help with what I'm going to tell you. And hey, again, I am sooooo sorry for last night. Really. Thanks for forgiving me."

"It's OK," said Dare. "I know you're at your wits end. You missed a great little mini-concert with Jamie and the

65

Hanks. But you absolutely would not believe what happened while that was going on."

Jo looked at him expectantly. "Well?" she said.

"They had just finished playing one set so it was kind of quiet. Well, I mean, it wasn't as noisy as it was when they were playing. So, me and a couple of the guys were just hanging around waiting for them to start up again. I see this guy out the corner of my eye coming from the lot, big guy with sandy-colored hair. Looks like he came from a burgundy work van because I hadn't seen that in the lot before."

It sounded like he was talking about Chris, but she had no idea why.

Dare looked out at the ocean and then back at Jo. She waited for him to go on.

"He stops and kind of surveys the crowd and then spies Rob Wingate leaning up against the crab pots on the dock. He walks right up to him and says something like 'Long time no see Rob.' Rob starts backin' up. He looked scared. I thought he was going to fall into the water."

Jo gasped with the realization she might know what happened next.

"I think I heard him say something like 'Chris, what brings you back here?' And this guy, Chris I guess, says, 'Think back a bit, Rob. You know damn well why I am here.' And then he, Chris, says something about a message and ruining his life and the next thing we all know, he winds up and punches Rob and Rob falls into the water just like that. He's sputtering and saying, 'It wasn't a big deal'." Dare shook his head in amazement.

"And that guy Chris just looks at him and says, 'Fuck you, Rob. It was a really big deal, you asshole.' He gets back into his van and drives away. It was crazy. Never seen someone take on ol' Rob like that. 'Bout time, though. But what do you make of that? Just a bit of comic relief, I 'spose, after the storm."

Jo stopped walking and looked straight at Dare. "You aren't going to believe this, but that man, that guy Chris, is probably my grandfather."

"Your grandfather?" Dare looked at her incredulously. "I thought your dad's dad lived somewhere far away. Why is he here? And how did he know Rob?

"No, Dare," Jo said. "Not my dad's dad. My mom's. The grandfather I never knew I had. The missing piece. The man messed up my mom and then me in a way all these years. He was a part of us when he wasn't a part of us at all. He influenced us, you know? I don't know what to think and I sure don't know what to do."

Jo was sobbing and Dare was totally perplexed. "What am I missing, Jo? There's something here I'm not getting. How do you know he's your grandfather and how did you meet this man? What's going on?"

Jo sank into his arms, still sobbing. "It all happened last night after you left Marcie's. There was one empty seat at the bar, where you were, and he sat there. We started talking and he said his same was Jonathan and he mentioned roofing and I told him we needed repairs at the motel and he said he'd been there before and I said the motel was in my family and somehow, I mentioned Gran's name and he got all weird and then he said he'd known her but she wouldn't want him working on the roof and then I found out his name was really Chris and then I fainted."

"You fainted?" gasped Dare. "Why?"

"Because Gran told me the night of the storm that Chris was the guy, the only guy, she was with that summer when she got pregnant. And when I came to and confronted him about abandoning her, he told me his dad had a heart attack and he had to leave in the middle of the night. He left a message with Rob...."

"And Rob never gave it to her," nodded Dare slowly. "So, that explains him coming to the dock, recognizing him, and punching him out."

"And all these years, my gran thought he'd left her and he thought she'd just cast him aside. He never knew about my mom, never knew about anything," Jo said.

"But why didn't he come back, try to contact her?" Dare asked. "It seems if he cared about her, he would have."

"Humph. If only life was so simple. I've thought about that. His mom was apparently in pieces after his dad got sick and then his dad died about a week later. He had to take over the family roofing business and take care of her. He kept waiting for Gran to call. But then she had her own issues by then, didn't she? And she had been told he'd left her for another girl. And she had no way to contact him, did she? Chris Smith from somewhere up north? Turns out, since he was living with his family, he wouldn't have had a phone of his own back then. Kids didn't have phones like we do now. Heck, Gran told me once the phones were connected to the walls! It would have been under his father's name anyway. Chris's first name isn't even Chris, it's Jonathan. And, by the way, he never married either."

Dare thought for a moment and then said, "Life hit them both really hard. It's like that hurricane hit them both and did damage neither of them really understood. It's hard to believe, but I guess given their circumstances back then, there wasn't much either of them could do."

"Yeah," said Jo. "And time passed and while they didn't forget about one another they both assumed they'd been forgotten by the other. Oh Dare – how do I handle this?

Clearly with Chris finding Rob last night and practically knocking him out, he had to have had some reason. You just don't go doing that. And you said he walked right toward him – he knew who Rob was."

"I'd say you're right, Jo," Dare agreed. "But your parents are coming today and you'll have to tell them, and what about your Gran? Did you tell her?"

"Hell, no," Jo explained. "I was so wiped out when I got home last night I couldn't think straight and I wasn't even sure I thought Chris was for real. Now with what you've told me, it seems more likely he really is my grandfather. But how do I handle this?"

She and Dare walked along, the silence only broken by the sound of the waves and the crying of the gulls. Everything seemed the same to Jo but at the same time everything was different. Then Dare turned to Jo.

"Look, I am no expert in any of this. But I think that being straight up with them is best. It's not the first time in history someone's relative has appeared from nowhere. With genetic testing these days it seems it's happening more and more. What they do with the information is up to them. And you'll have to decide what you want to do. Accept Chris or not. Try to build a relationship or not. And you have to realize your mom and gran might feel differently. You might all choose to handle this differently. And the three of you all have your own issues. I don't envy you, Jo, I really don't. But I am happy at least you know who your grandfather is."

"Me too, Dare. Me too. My gran said a few things to me last night that I need to really take to heart. And maybe if I can try to work on things with Mom, I can get her to work on things with Gran. But I know I'll have to tell them about Chris. I think one at a time. I'll tell Mom first, and then we can tell Gran together. Chris is supposed to get in touch with me and I will have to ask him to keep his distance. But then I'm assuming he wants to meet them. He didn't have a choice about meeting me. I just appeared to him as suddenly as he appeared to me."

"Well, you've got a few hours to think about it," said Dare, looking at his phone. "It's almost eight and you need to go home and then get back to the motel by eight-thirty. And I sure need to be at the docks. A few of the boats are about ready to take on charters when the island re-opens for guests and I'm going to be there to mate. I'm not giving up on my dream of getting my captain's license but I've got to put in my time. You know that. I'm really close to the seven hundred twenty hours."

"I do know that, Dare. That's awesome. Thanks for listening." She smiled at him. "And I'll text you today. I'm not sure where Chris will be on the island, but I hope he'll find time to get in touch. He promised me he would." Sighing, she added, "My next challenge arrives around noon. Wish me luck."

"You don't need luck, Jo. You'll figure this out." They were back at the motel. Dare waved as he hopped into his truck. Jo waved back and pedaled back to the breakfast she knew Gran had waiting. It would have to be a quick one.

I want this to work out, Jo thought as she pedaled along. *But are happy endings really possible in life? I guess there are at least four of us who will determine that.*

Chapter Seven

The phone was ringing when Jo arrived at the office and it didn't stop for the next hour. People were anxious to re-book their vacations shortened by the storm, and Labor Day reservations were strong. Focusing on the motel and the work at hand surprisingly allowed her mind to clear a bit regarding Chris, her parents, and her grandmother. She wasn't exactly sure how this would all play out, but she felt she would know what to do when the time came. In the meantime, she double-checked with the housekeepers that every room was in order, and she asked them to pay particular attention to the room her parents would be staying in. She wanted her mom to be pleased with how quickly they had recovered from the storm, and how hard she had worked to that end.

She walked over to the oceanfront and leaned over the railing for a few minutes. The beautiful sunrise had morphed into an equally beautiful morning, and the day was going to be one of those late summer gems. The humidity had dropped, the breeze was warm and gentle, and the colors of the water were like paintings she had seen, greens and blues of every hue. She loved this place, there was no denying it. And she loved her studies at the university. She could hardly wait to get back into the lab and eventually into the fieldwork, although she had done plenty of her own fieldwork and research over the years right here. Jellyfish amazed her. They didn't frighten her; to the contrary, she felt like she could handle them endlessly – although a few stings early on made her that much wiser as she grew up. It occurred to her that even with the storm delay for fall classes, she'd only be on the island for a few more weeks. Gran was well on the mend, and she'd take care of everything as they moved into the off-season.

Her phone pinged with a text. She looked down and saw it was from her mom.

"At Whalebone. Quick stop here. Be there in an hour."

"OK," she texted back. Then she thought for a second and added, *"Can't wait to see you!"*

She was sure that would surprise her mom, but she had decided she would extend the olive branch. Deep down inside, she wanted things to be more normal between them. She did love her. It just seemed through her teen years and when she left for college it was easier to keep that wall up and pretend that she didn't care. Somehow, she thought she should hold that resentment forever. But lately, and especially after what Gran had said, she realized she was being very stubborn and maybe foolish. How much easier the conversations ahead would be if only she had realized all of this years ago. Now there were two major issues that had to be addressed.

She knew how quickly an hour could fly in the office, so she hurried back and took care of the few emails and voice mails that had come in during her brief break. It seemed more like ten minutes when she heard footsteps coming up the stairway to the office. She rose and stepped out from behind the counter to greet her parents, her heart beating so hard she was sure they'd see it beneath her T-shirt.

"Mom, Dad," she exclaimed. "Got here OK, I see." Her dad grinned, gave her a warm hug. He stepped back and Jo hesitated only a fraction of a second before she reached out to her mom. "So, you can see we didn't blow away, mom," she said, putting her arms around SeaAnna.

"Well, so I see," sputtered SeaAnna. "To what do I owe such a warm welcome?"

"I, uh, just know you were worried," said Jo, trying to maintain her cheery demeanor. "I mean, it was a pretty nasty storm. We've been working hard to get everything together for re-opening. I don't think the losses will hurt us too much. Gran's been looking at the numbers, and she thinks August will not be far off target."

"Well, that's good to know," said SeaAnna carefully. "And how is she?"

"Doing much better," Jo replied. "She's anxious to see you." Jo knew Susan had as much trepidation as she did about this visit, but she thought it wouldn't hurt to try to set things up on a positive note as much as possible.

"JoBell, it is great to see how quickly everything got

73

back together," her dad said. "I'd like to take a walk around the property with you as soon as we get settled in. Just to see how the oceanfront held up and all. The TV images we saw were rough, but I guess different parts of the island were impacted differently."

"For sure," Jo agreed. "Some of the homes and buildings near the docks didn't fare nearly as well and the soundside flooding really messed up a lot of houses in Frisco. You'll see them when we drive around. But let me help you with your stuff, and then we'll take that walk."

She smiled at her mom, who looked at her uncertainly, and then headed out the door ahead of her parents. "Just take the car across the street and park right under where your room is. You're in two-ten in Building C. I'll meet you over there."

Mike and SeaAnna drove to where Jo had indicated and began unloading. "I'm not sure how long we'll be here," said SeaAnna. "Just long enough, I suppose, to check on mom and be sure things are in order here. "

Jo looked at what they had brought and realized her mom was speaking truthfully. Just one suitcase for the two of them and a small overnight bag was all she saw. Clearly, they weren't intending to stay any length of time. *But why would they?* she thought to herself. *It's not like they expect us to have a warm family reunion.*

She must have been frowning because her dad said, "Well, we didn't bring all that much because we knew you'd have it all under control, Jo. No doubt."

Jo again forced a smile. "Gran said something about a late lunch early dinner kind of thing at the house. Even though she's hobbling a bit, she can still cook. That will give you time to rest, Mom. And Dad, we can take that inspection tour."

"So solicitous," said SeaAnna slowly. "Anything I'm missing here?"

"Not a thing, Mom," said Jo. "Such a beautiful day, I know a good sit on the porch with a rocker would be so relaxing. I know it's what you like to do." She placed the luggage by the door and unlocked it. "Ta da! Your room awaits."

Mike and SeaAnna walked in and her mom simply nodded her approval. "Yes, Jo, I think I would like an hour or two just to relax. Mike, I can get everything out and put up. Go on out with her and stretch your legs."

"Tell you what, Jo. I'll be back over to the office in fifteen minutes and we'll make the rounds. OK?" Mike asked.

"Sure," she responded. "Since there are no guests here yet, I'll lock up the office and we can take our time. Gran doesn't expect us until around at least four or so." She realized an opportunity had just presented itself, and so for now, step one was pretty clear. She'd talk to her dad first and see what he suggested.

She barely had time to get back to the office and take a few more phone calls when she saw her dad start across the highway. She hoped he'd noticed her small efforts to be more civilized and even kind to her mom.

He had. "Jo, I noticed that your attitude toward your mom has changed a bit," he said as they stepped off the porch and began walking around all of the buildings on the soundside. "Not sure what brought that on, but it is overdue, you know? And she did notice as well. She's uncertain as to your motives, but I think she's pleased. I know she's mulling this all over while we take our little tour here."

"Dad, there is no ulterior motive. I've done a lot of thinking, and Gran really talked to me the other night.

When it comes right down to it, I've held a stupid grudge since I was a teen, and I keep acting like that same adolescent. Time to grow up. Plus, I miss what I think we should have in terms of a relationship. And I have been thinking about this for a long time, but now there's a really big reason that she and I need to be able to talk and care for one another."

Mike stopped short and looked at her carefully. "Why do you say that, Jo? Are you sick? Is there something wrong with your grandmother beyond the twisted ankle?"

"No, it's not that." Jo took a deep breath and returned his stare as she said, "Dad, Mom's father is here. My grandfather. Your father-in-law. He's on this island. Now. It is a crazy story but you have to hear me out and then you have to help me with Mom. And with Gran. They have to know and you have to help me tell them. I know you probably don't believe me but it's true." Jo realized she was feeling light-headed and she worried she might faint again so she sat on the steps to the pool and Mike quickly sat down beside her.

"Jo, what are you saying? This isn't some kind of joke, is it? If you are trying to make up to your mom with a stunt like this, it's not going to work. How and why would you come up with a story like this?" Mike asked sternly, his voice so sharp it caught Jo by surprise.

"Listen, Dad, and I'll tell you. But let me get through it all first before you interrupt," Jo pleaded. Mike nodded.

She then related everything that had happened in the past twenty-four hours from her small spat with Dare, to Chris occupying the empty chair, their ensuing conversation and her realization that this was the same Chris her grandmother had told her about the night of the storm.

"Sorry but I have to interrupt," said Mike a bit incredulously. "Your grandmother told you all about her relationship with this guy, this man, back in nineteen seventy-five?"

"She did. She wanted to. I guess with this storm being so reminiscent of that one, it brought a lot of feelings to the surface. We were just keeping one another company and talking to try to keep our thoughts from the storm. She felt I was old enough to hear it. She was pretty matter of fact and I don't judge her. She was my age when all that happened and she was dealt a pretty rough hand with getting pregnant, Great Grandma and Great Granddad getting sick, taking care of them until they passed, and raising Mom and not being able to finish college. And then, she thought that Chris had up and left her for someone else. But he had a different story when I confronted him."

She continued to tell the story, and finished with what Dare had told her about Chris showing up at the docks and punching Rob Wingate. "And so, I can't imagine why he would just show up out of the blue and do that if what he said wasn't true. This was all one horrendous mix-up with him and Gran. "

Mike sat motionless for several moments. "How did you leave things with him, Jo?"

"I gave him my cell number and asked him to please keep in touch with me. Honestly, Dad, when I first figured things out, I wanted to kill him I was so angry. But the more we talked and I heard what he had to say, I, well, he's really not a bad guy, I don't think. My guess is he has a lot to think about now too."

"That's for sure," said Mike. "Let me mull this over while we walk around a bit more. I really do want to see how this place survived the storm."

He was very quiet as Jo took him by the pool, and then

over to the oceanfront units. She was proud to let him see that things were very much back in order.

"Obviously, the roof is the one remaining issue, and I know that can get fixed, just have to find the right company. There are several on the island now, so it will get handled in the next week or so. That will be OK, don't you think? Dad, are you listening?"

Mike was staring off into the horizon. He slowly turned to Jo and said, "I'll tell you what I think. I think that before you say a word to your Mom or Susan, I need to find him and speak to him. I want to meet him, and I want to see what he's thinking. Could be he doesn't want to have any contact with any of us. In which case, there's nothing further to say. But if he does, well, the three of us will need to think of what to do next. I wonder how I can find him?"

"He drives a burgundy work van with 'JCS Roofing' in white lettering on the side. I guess with all the commercial roofing issues here, if you drive around, you'll spot him pretty quickly," Jo said as they walked back across the parking lot toward the office.

"I don't think I'll need to drive around," said Mike. Jo looked at him quizzically as he pointed to the motel next door. "If I'm not mistaken, that's the van right there."

Sure enough, the van and another work truck similarly marked were in the lot not one hundred yards away from where they now stood. Mike started to walk that way and Jo cried out, "Right now?"

"No time like the present," said Mike. Jo watched him walk for a few moments and then ducked inside the office. Things were moving very quickly, but Dare had said it was best to confront all this head-on. Head-on was one thing, a head-on collision was another. What would her dad say? What would Chris say?

She looked at the wall clock. It was half past one. They wouldn't be expected at Gran's until around four or four-thirty. Surely, her dad wouldn't be gone that long. Was her mom taking a nap? Would she realize Mike was gone a little longer than necessary for the motel "tour"? He was checking in with a roofing company, she could say. That wasn't entirely false.

She realized there was nothing further she could do until her dad came back with whatever information he had, so she started going through emails. It seemed the island would open up to guests in two days. Her phone pinged and there was a message from Dare.

Everything ok?

Jo: *Not sure. I told my Dad.*

Dare: *Really? And?*

Jo: *He's over talking to Chris now. Chris is working next door. Whoa. Dad's coming back. Gotta go. Later.*

Jo saw her dad striding back across the highway and heading for the office. He hadn't been gone but about twenty minutes, although it seemed like much longer to Jo.

"What happened?" Jo asked. She was not at all certain what to expect.

"Well, that was probably the most interesting and awkward conversation I've ever had in my life," said Mike. "I will agree with you, he is a decent man, or seems to be. At first, he didn't believe me when I told him I was your father. But once we got that sorted out, he confirmed pretty much everything you told me. Except you conveniently left out the part where you fainted at Marcie's."

"I didn't want you to think I was being too dramatic, Dad," Jo said. "But do you believe him? Do you believe me?"

"Yes, I do," Mike admitted. "And there's something else you didn't mention, which maybe you can't see but I can. There's an awful lot of him in your mom and in you. Especially in the way you all smile. If that's not a family resemblance, I don't know what is."

"But does he want to meet Mom and Gran? Does he want to keep in touch with me?" Jo asked. She suddenly knew that she wanted the answer to be yes more than she could have anticipated.

"He's not sure, Jo, to be honest," said Mike. "He's a bit in shock and that's never a good time to make any hard and fast decisions. I told him you and I would be telling your mom and grandmother today. I have no idea how they will take this news. You need to be prepared for anything." He squeezed her arm. "I'm going back to the room to try to rest a bit. I'm going to feign fatigue from the drive but I'm really going to think about how we handle this."

Mike stepped out onto the porch, then stuck his head back in. "Oh, and don't worry about the roof. No matter what, he'll do the job. I'll take care of working it out in case the rest of this goes haywire. He said he'd feel terrible if someone else did it. So, you can cross that one off your list."

That was the easy one, Jo thought. *The rest of this is going to be a whole lot harder.*

Chapter Eight

Dinner had gone surprisingly well, and now Jo and her mom did the dishes while Mike and Susan sat on the couches in the large open kitchen, dining, and living room area. The late afternoon was turning into early evening and the light was calming as it streamed through the windows. Jo tried to keep things light through dinner with small talk about different jellyfish she'd found throughout the summer, interesting guests they'd hosted at the motel including one minor TV star and an astronaut, and Dare's work toward his captain's license.

"That scampi was fantastic as always, Gran," Jo said as she finished washing the last pot and let the sink drain. "Fresh shrimp, wasn't it?"

"Yes," replied Susan. "The neighbor boy, what's his name? Tom or Tim?"

"Terrence, Gran," laughed Jo. "You never can remember his name."

"Well, whatever," smiled Susan. "His dad had caught some and he had the little guy bring some over. Nice of them. They've turned out to be real good neighbors over the years. Sweet family, all of them." Susan maneuvered her ankle on the couch and turned to Jo. " Honey, would you open the new bottle of wine? It would be nice to sit here for a while and just chat."

Susan and Jo had both noticed SeaAnna had been quiet and they were hoping they could extend their own family time a bit longer, though each for different reasons. Susan was just enjoying a rare moment of the four of them together. Jo knew what was just ahead, and didn't want SeaAnna to decide to leave now.

"I'll get it, Gran. Mom, Dad? Want a glass? And do you mind if I have some?" Jo asked as she grabbed the bottle from the fridge and rummaged around a drawer for the opener.

"Why ask?" queried SeaAnna. "Surely, you must be drinking now."

"Actually, I'm not, Mom," replied Jo. "I might have a glass with Gran now and then, but otherwise, it's lemonade at Marcie's or anywhere else. Guess I'm strange that way. But if you don't mind, I'm pouring myself one too."

She gave each of them a glass. "Dad, why don't you make a toast?"

Mike stood and looked at the three women sitting there

expectantly. He knew Jo had given him an opening and so he began slowly, "Here's to three strong women, Jo's excellent work after the storm, Susan's recovery from her ankle, and SeaAnna for being my wonderful wife. And also, for family."

They toasted and each took a sip. For Jo, it was more of a gulp but she hoped no one noticed. It was quiet for a few moments and then Mike began, "Speaking of family..."

"Were we?" SeaAnna interrupted.

"Yes, in a way," said Mike. "There's something that's happened that is going to change our family in possibly a big way."

Susan and SeaAnna immediately looked at Jo. "No, you're not pregnant, Jo?" her mother gasped.

Jo wanted to laugh but it was hardly the time. "No, I am not," she said flatly.

SeaAnna sat back into the couch and looked up at Mike who was still standing. "So then, what in the world are you talking about?"

"SeaAnna and Susan," he began. "Jo is going to tell you a story. And I'm going to ask you not to interrupt her until she is done, as difficult as that may be. What she's going to tell you is true, but it goes against what you both think you know. And it might hurt and I'm sure it will confuse you both. But please, hear her out and then I'll add my two cents' worth."

He sat down and Jo took another rather large sip of wine. So, this was it. Head-on, Dare had said. She looked over at Susan and said, "Remember when you asked me why I was a bit late coming from Marcie's last night? Well, Dare and I had a spat, that's true. But that lasted only a short time and he left. Someone sat next to me while I was there, drinking lemonade, Mom, and waiting for my takeout order to finish. And we started talking..."

Jo relayed what happened next, her mother looking increasingly agitated and Susan's face unreadable. Skipping over her fainting spell, she knew the penny had already dropped for Susan as Jo heard her sharp intake of breath. Jo quickly went through her confrontation with Chris and his response, but she had started to cry and she worried she wasn't making much sense at all. She added what Dare had told her about the incident with Rob Wingate at the docks and then looked pleadingly at her father to continue.

But before he could, SeaAnna stood up and said, "That's enough. I don't want to hear any more. I don't believe it. This guy could be anybody, really, lots of people have those initials. You probably led him on in the conversation Jo, and so he was just answering you like you wanted him to."

"SeaAnna, please, sit," said Mike. "I've spoken to him. He thinks maybe DNA testing is in order even though he understands what happened and he's not denying anything."

"Oh, he wants testing, does he?" Susan suddenly spoke out, her face red and her eyes glaring. "Thinks there was someone else after him? He's a son of a bitch, and if it is him, I'll have nothing to do with him." Her eyes went to her granddaughter. "Jo, there's brandy in the cabinet above the fridge. Please pour me some. Now."

Jo did as she was told but SeaAnna was railing at Mike. "When did you see him? What did you say? How can you be so sure?"

"I'm not totally certain, SeaAnna. Please calm down a bit. This is not a conversation I ever thought I'd be having and I'm sure I'm doing it all wrong but I think he is your father and Jo's grandfather and we need to figure this out reasonably. He told me he'd already had testing done because his mother's family had a crazy lineage and he wanted to know more about it."

"Wait a minute," SeaAnna interrupted again. "Jo, you did testing as part of a class you took, didn't you? And no connections were made. So, that settles that."

"Mom," Jo said gently. "I don't know what test Chris took but there are a few companies out there doing DNA testing, so it's possible we used different companies and then we wouldn't have been connected. Dad, any chance he told you the company name?"

"He did, it's the one you see on TV all the time. If you tell me the name, I'd remember. It's Family, um..."

"Family Tree," said Jo. "And I took my test through Exploring Heritage. So, they are different. Mom, would you get tested?"

"I would not," SeaAnna stated flatly. "I think this conversation has gone far enough. Mike, I want to go back to the motel. Jo, we'll be checking out in the morning." She stood up and began walking toward to door.

"Mom," Jo cried out. "Please don't be angry with me. I knew this would be an unbelievable shock but I don't want to be blamed for this. I thought you and Gran should know. Dad thought you should know." Tears were flowing freely now and she went over to hug SeaAnna but SeaAnna did not respond except to say, "So this was why you were so friendly to me today. And here I thought it was an honest expression, but you were trying to soften me up for this blow. Mike, please, I'd like to go now."

"And I'm going to bed," said Susan without expression. She had been lost in the drama but now Jo, Mike, and SeaAnna saw that the one person who might be the most impacted had said almost nothing to this point. She had known and loved Chris Smith. Jo and SeaAnna only knew of his existence in some distant way. "Jo, don't disturb me. I don't want to see him, if it is him. I find it difficult to believe the story about Rob, scumbag that he is. He probably can't remember yesterday let alone that summer. Just because you think this man is the Chris I knew, doesn't mean he is. I have nothing more to say and, Jo, I'm serious, leave me alone tonight."

Jo opened her mouth but the look she got from her dad made her close it and just nod in reply. Susan limped slightly down the hallway and shut the door. When Jo looked back, her mom was already halfway down the steps. Mike stood on the landing, arms open to her, and Jo walked over, needing that hug badly.

"Oh Dad, that was awful," she sobbed.

"JoBell, what could you possibly have expected? This is not just a bombshell, it's like an atomic bomb of news. I think you told me Dare said that each of you had to react in your own way. And you are. And they will. Give your mom and grandmother some time. They may see things differently tomorrow or they may not. Either way, we just have to wait." He rubbed his hand behind her back. It was soothing and she was calming down a bit. "And I think your grandmother was pretty firm about not being disturbed. So, don't do it. They both have all the facts as much as we know them. Now they have to deal with their emotions. Try to get some sleep yourself. I'll see you in the morning."

"But Mom said you're leaving," she said softly.

"Not sure about that," replied Mike. "But let me handle your mom."

He kissed her on the forehead and continued, "And don't dwell on what your mom just said. She is totally upset and you're an easy target for her to lash out on. I know you've just worked through some stuff in your head and heart with her. Try to let this go and please keep trying, because it's going to be worth it. OK?"

Jo hugged him again and waved as he walked down the steps and got into the car. She watched them drive away and felt more miserable than she had in a long time. The house had seemed almost happy during dinner and now it felt empty and cold. She walked up to her grandmother's door but heard sobbing, and realized that her dad was right. This was not the time for her to interfere.

She got into bed and tossed and turned for hours, working out scenarios in her head until she was exhausted. She finally fell into a restless sleep, her dreams a jumble of the people in her life, all of them bobbing up and down in a stormy ocean with jellyfish all around them.

When she awoke at six thirty, she felt tired and sad. She showered quickly and noticed that Gran's door was still closed. She tiptoed into the kitchen and grabbed her usual yogurt. She found a piece of paper and wrote, "I love you, Gran," and added a big heart and a rough drawing of a smiling jellyfish. Then she exited the house and made her way to the motel. If nothing else, with the island re-opening tomorrow to tourists, she would have a busy day and that was probably a good thing.

She was thinking of how she really didn't even have a chance to say goodbye to her parents when she pedaled into the parking lot and was surprised to see their car in its space on the oceanside. She was equally surprised when, not long after she turned on the "Open" sign and checked the phone and computer for messages, her dad appeared, coming up the steps.

"Mornin', Jo" he smiled at her. "How did you sleep? Can you get me a cup of coffee?"

"I thought you'd be on the road by now, for sure. I'm surprised," Jo said.

"Your mom and I were up for a long time last night as you might have imagined. We talked until the wee hours and so she's still asleep. I didn't want to mess with the coffee in the room, so I thought I'd grab some here. You still have the coffeemaker for guests, don't you?"

"It's good that you reminded me. Probably need to put in some fresh water and all. Haven't used it since before the storm," she replied. She busied herself with cleaning the pot and getting the coffee brewed. "So, you'll leave when she wakes up? You'll stop by, won't you?"

"Actually," said Mike, taking the mug from her. "We're not leaving today. And she said once she gets up and dressed and has her coffee, she'd like to have some time with you, just the two of you. And before you start thinking of everything bad it could be, I think she just wants to talk to you and start to make things right. I assured her you weren't setting her up yesterday, and we went through everything again last night in painstaking detail. And she has some news for you. So, I'll man the ship here while you talk. I have no clue what to do but I can manage."

Jo let what her dad had said sink in for a moment before she answered him.

"I appreciate that, Dad, but today will be crazy with the island re-opening tomorrow. Let me see if I can call Lauren and get her to come in. She's worked part-time for most of the summer, but since the storm, I haven't had to call her in. She'll be happy for the money." She appeased her dad, "Not that you can't handle it, but she knows the system. It will give you a chance to just drive around the island and survey things. Maybe you can go down to the docks. Dare will be getting ready for charters booked from tomorrow on, but I'm sure he'd like to see you."

Jo got out her phone and waited for Lauren to answer. She explained that she needed to be away for a few hours and would Lauren mind coming in around ten? She flashed her dad the "thumbs up" sign, thanked Lauren profusely, and hung up.

"She said she could be here and can work as long as need be. She doesn't have children and her husband works on the ferry, so she's got plenty of time today," Jo said. "I'll be here until then. Tell Mom I'll come over as soon as Lauren gets here and I'll try to keep an open mind."

Jo gave Mike a grateful smile. " I am really happy you're not leaving, Dad. And I want this to be a good conversation with Mom no matter what she is thinking about Chris."

Mike smiled again. "That's a good attitude to have, Jo," he said. "I'm going to head over to that breakfast place just down the street and have a big breakfast because I know your mom wouldn't approve. The scampi last night was terrific but I'm hungry again as usual. And the yogurt you two eat just doesn't cut it for me."

Jo allowed herself to laugh a bit. "She has always tried to keep you nice and thin, Dad. And it's working. So, I think a big breakfast now and then won't hurt."

The office phone began to ring. Mike nodded to her and headed out and Jo settled into the office routine. She was amazed when Lauren walked through the door.

"Aren't you early?" she asked Lauren.

"Well, if you call ten minutes to ten early, I guess I am," Lauren replied.

"Oh, good grief. I can't believe it's almost ten. This morning has been unreal. Let me go over a few things with you so you'll be up to speed. Tomorrow we will be nearly full. Can you believe it?"

She quickly caught Lauren up with messages left, return calls expected, housekeeping assignments, and small maintenance issues that Art, the maintenance man, was tending to.

"Take all the time you need, Jo," Lauren told Jo. "I can be here until closing. Enjoy your parents. Special times."

Jo nodded. "I'll text you and keep you posted. Thanks again." Then she started across the road for her conversation with SeaAnna. It was another gorgeous day and that helped to lift her spirits. She knocked on the door of her parents' room and SeaAnna opened it but immediately stepped out onto the porch.

"I thought it was such a lovely day, we'd just take a nice walk on the beach," SeaAnna said. "You don't mind, do you?"

"No, not at all," Jo replied. She was glad to be out in the fresh air, more in her element by the ocean and its calming waves. "I hope you got some sleep. Dad said you kept late hours last night."

"We did," SeaAnna said as they made their way from the steps to the beach. "Jo, I had, and still have, so much to process." SeaAnna sighed. "I see how you are with your dad. You know, I've never experienced those feelings, those emotions. I don't know what it's like to have a dad." SeaAnna stopped and placed her hands on Jo's shoulders.

"I've missed so much. And it was always so easy to blame him, the father I didn't know." Dropping her arms, SeaAnna resumed her walk and Jo followed.

After a few seconds, SeaAnna said, "Now I find out there's really no one to blame, it was all just one big communications breakdown. I don't know how to feel."

She took her hand and brushed a loose strand of hair from Jo's face. "But one thing I do know is that you and I, we need to make a fresh start. Somewhere along the way, I messed up on the mother-daughter thing and I need to fix that. But I don't know how I messed up and I need you to tell me where I went wrong."

"You didn't go wrong, Mom," Jo answered. "I was the one who went wrong. And for a very stupid reason. Do you remember when I was twelve or thirteen we had this big fight?"

"We did?" SeaAnna looked like she was concentrating hard. "I don't think I remember that."

"We were really going at each other, screaming back and forth. I know I said some things I regret and then you told me something I could never look past."

"I did? What did I say?"

Almost whispering, eyes on the sand below her feet, Jo said, "You told me I was a mistake. "SeaAnna gasped, but Jo wasn't done yet. She needed to say this, she needed to know. "You said that you'd never wanted kids. That you'd messed up with your birth control or something." Tears were now streaming down Jo's face as she remembered that day and the pain that was still so raw. "You said you were a mistake for Gran and now you'd made a similar mistake with me."

"I'm sorry," Sea Anna tried to say through the tears that ran down her face. But Jo wasn't listening.

"I remember as soon as you said it, you stopped and tried to apologize but I just couldn't ever forgive or forget what you said."

SeaAnna looked at Jo intently, both visibly trying to contain the emotions running through them. "I really said that?"

"Yeah. I don't even remember what the fight was about

anymore. But you said that. I was just never able to forget it. It hurt a lot. And as days and weeks and months passed, the angrier and more hurt I got until I decided that I just didn't want to be with you or talk to you or really have anything to do with you. You said you were sorry but I just didn't believe it."

SeaAnna walked for several minutes before turning to Jo. "If I tell you I have no memory of that incident, you may not believe me. But, Jo, I don't. Moms and teenage girls argue all the time and say things they don't mean. How could you possibly be a mistake? I'm so proud of you and who you are, what you do, and how you have stepped up with the responsibility of the motel this summer. Do you mean that one argument is what this has been about all these years?"

Now it was Jo's turn to walk along silently. Then she spoke. "I guess that's what started it. But I always felt like you were trying to push me away, to boarding school and then to camps and whatnot and then here for the summers."

"But I thought you enjoyed school," said SeaAnna. "It gave you a great head start for college, look at where you are now after just one year. You're way ahead and doing great. And I thought you enjoyed the camps too. You made friends so easily. Not at all like me. And please don't tell me you didn't enjoy the summers with your Gran."

Jo smiled. She rarely heard her mother use Jo's pet name for her grandmother.

"No, you're right," she said. "The summers here helped mold me and give me direction and purpose. I love it here, Mom, even if you don't. But you're also right that I kept holding on to what you said for way too long, and I never talked with you about it. And in the meantime, we just seemed to grow further apart and then that seemed to be normal. But it's not normal, and I want normal again."

"Do you?" asked SeaAnna. "Because I do too. You have no idea how I've missed you. It seemed you despised me for reasons I just didn't understand." SeaAnna shook her head. "Another communication breakdown. Seems it's the season. But this is one we can fix and we can start now."

She stopped and hugged Jo tightly. "It's not going to be easy but we can try. Together. Would that work for you?"

Jo wiped the tear from her mom's face and then did the same to her own. They both stood there in the morning sun crying and then laughing.

"What people must be thinking," Jo laughed harder. "They don't know they are witnessing the reconciliation of the century right here and now!" Then she paused for a minute and said, "Mom, at the risk of ruining this beautiful morning, I hope maybe you can try to make up with Gran too. I don't know what has kept the two of you apart all these years. Maybe it's time for you two to talk. I didn't see her last night but I heard her crying. And she didn't get up with me this morning like she always does. It seems to me that maybe you have blamed her for things over which she had no control, like your dad not being in the picture. I don't know. It's just a thought."

SeaAnna slowly nodded in agreement. "That's something else your dad and I talked about last night. She's getting older. You may not see it but I do. And I realize time is going by and I haven't had have any kind of relationship with my mother or my daughter. Something is very wrong with that picture. So, I'm trying to make it all better. Maybe not overnight, but in time. And whatever I think about Chris, whether or not he really is my dad, doesn't matter.

She loved him once and felt betrayed for all these years. I should be there for her."

"So," said Jo slowly. "What are you going to do?"

"I'm going over to see her this afternoon. Hopefully, she'll let me in and we can have a good talk, a good cry, or both. And then I will tell her my decision."

"What decision is that?" Jo asked, remembering that her dad had told her something about her mom having news to share.

"I'm going to get the DNA test," said SeaAnna. "I wrestled with it all night but we'll never know, will we? Unless you do it and I don't think you should have to. I am the daughter and it's my responsibility. We need to know. Then we can all move forward however we feel." Looking out at sea for a few seconds, SeaAnna remained silent.

"Jo, I'm not going to tell you what to do or feel. You are an adult now. If you want to maintain communication with Chris, you can. And if the test comes back and we're not related, well, you'll have to just count him as a friend. But if he is my father and your grandfather, that's different."

"Are you going to meet him," Jo asked.

"No, I don't think so. Not now. I want to get the test results back. It gives me time. I need time."

Jo wanted to disagree, but when she looked at SeaAnna, she saw a woman who was really struggling. Jo wasn't going to argue the point. SeaAnna had more than enough on her plate. She decided to switch subjects for the moment. They turned and began walking back toward the motel, by now just a speck in the distance.

"Mom, I have to ask you, did you know where your name came from? That you were named after a boat?" Jo asked.

"Someone told me back in the day at school," admitted

SeaAnna. "So, I never had to ask Mom. I wasn't sure what the connection was, but since it's such a strange name, I figured it was true and I didn't want details. As you well know since we just discussed this, teen years are hell. I wasn't very nice to your gran, then or now."

"But you're going to see her and that's great. I'm going to take Dad out to dinner later so we'll be well out of the way. You take as long as you want or need. We'll be fine."

Jo glanced at her phone. They had walked for a long time and it was nearly noon.

"I'm going to let Lauren run the office this afternoon. I want to think about everything too. I've got a bathing suit at the office and I'm just going to soak up the sun out here on the beach. Haven't had much time to truly enjoy this place lately and school is going to start again soon. I'm waiting on the official e-mail but I'm guessing it will be in ten days or so. And I'll need time to get home and pack up."

They walked the rest of the way in silence. When they got to SeaAnna's room, Jo spoke carefully. "Mom, I am so, so, so sorry for these years. We can't get them back, but if you accept my apology, can we, um, be friends?"

SeaAnna smiled and Jo saw Chris all over her face. "I think we can be mother-daughter and I think that's even better than friends. Go on and try to relax this afternoon. If I don't see you later, we will see you tomorrow, for sure. We do have to leave. Your dad has to get back to the office. He has clients to meet and Zoom won't cut it for this project."

"And I have people coming into your room," Jo added. "Hate to have to kick you out."

They shared a laugh together, for the first time in a very long time. Jo felt good as she walked back to the office. Then she heard, and then saw, people on the roof. Her dad met her on the office porch.

"Did it go OK?" he asked cautiously.

"Yes, it did," said Jo. "Fresh start time. But what is going on with the roof?"

"Funny thing," said Mike. "I ran into Chris at breakfast. He said he had finished the work next door earlier than he expected and he'd get his guys on our place today. Once they got here and took a look, they said it's mostly cosmetic and it won't take long at all. Probably done tonight if not first thing tomorrow." He smiled. "And he won't let the motel pay. I couldn't make him budge on that. Not sure of his reasons but I didn't argue."

"I guess that's OK. Not sure what to tell Gran but that's for another day," Jo said.

"Just tell her the truth when she asks. She's not going to go onto the roof and tear the new shingles off," Mike said. "Chris will likely be well away by the time she's back on the property, or at least he'll be working somewhere else, so it will be, as you know I love to say, done and dusted."

"Yes, you do love that saying," laughed Jo. "So, I'm going to spend my day on the beach and Mom told me she's going to talk to Gran. What will you do?"

"Drive around a bit more. I went north this morning after breakfast and checked things out. Now I'll take your earlier suggestion and head south down to the docks. Probably catch a bite to eat there."

"Boy, you're in luck Mom's occupied. She'd be all over you for eating a big breakfast and lunch. I thought you and I could meet at Marcie's for dinner say around six?" He nodded his agreement. "Good. I'll shower here so I don't disturb Mom and Gran. Pick me up here and save some room for Marcie's great shrimp basket."

This time, Mike gave her the "thumbs up" and walked back over to the oceanfront. Jo assumed he'd drop SeaAnna off at her grandmother's and then head on to the docks. She checked in with Lauren to make sure everything was OK, changed into her suit, and headed out for the beach. She hoped the salt air would clear her mind and allow her to think through things. She felt more settled about her mom for the moment, but exactly how did she feel about Chris?

Chapter Nine

Dare was busy at the docks that afternoon. Even though the island was just re-opening the next day, they already had an in-shore charter booked for that afternoon. And despite the fact he'd been working every day since the storm, a lot of that time had been on clean-up and helping everyone else getting things back in order.

Now it was time to really focus on the *Carefree,* the boat he mated on. Captain Jeff Neal was a good guy to work for, and his boat was the pride of the Hatteras Fleet. Not only was she a beautiful boat, she was large, at fifty feet. One of the largest in the area. She had large inboard diesels and the on-board technology was state-of-the art. But a beautiful boat doesn't guarantee success in catching fish. Captain Neal, like Dare, was born and raised on the island and knew the waters. He knew the baits, the lures, the currents, and the weather. It was no surprise that day in and day out his guests were all smiles when they pulled back into the docks late in the afternoon and proudly displayed the day's catch on the dock floor.

As Dare polished the rails and made certain everything was absolutely spotless, he once again found himself daydreaming about the day he, too, would own a boat like this one. Jeff Neal was a good friend of Dare's dad. They'd gone to school together. Jeff had started out mating. But he had come into some money when his Uncle Terry had passed away. Being the only male heir in the family, that helped him buy his first boat, a much smaller one than the *Carefree*. But it was that little boat that he made his reputation with, and from there, he just kept working his way up to larger boats and a client base that was the envy of plenty of the other captains. Dare wasn't automatically given the mate's position because of his dad, he had to earn it. Dare knew that he had and he was proud of that fact. A lot of the guys at the dock would like to mate on the *Carefree*.

Dare stood up to stretch, and noticed someone walking along the docks a few boats away from where *Carefree* was moored. As the man got closer, Dare realized with a start it was Chris Smith, the man who had decked Rob Wingate and who just might be, and probably was, Jo's grandfather.

Dare acknowledged him as he began walking by, but then he stopped to admire the *Carefree*. Not surprising, nearly everyone who visited the docks noticed her and took in her sleek lines and tall tower.

"This is one hell of a boat," said Chris. Dare stepped up out of the boat and onto the dock.

"She is that and more," said Dare proudly. "Often been said she's the pride of the Hatteras Fleet."

"I can see why. But do you catch fish?"

"There's probably not another captain who knows more about these waters than Captain Jeff Neal. So yes, we catch a lot of fish and we have plenty of satisfied customers. You may need to book a charter sometime if you can find a spot. Island opens up tomorrow and we're already booked solid for the next several weeks."

"Is that a fact? Jeff Neal, you said? I mated for a Captain Terry Neal once upon a time on his boat, the *SeaAnna*. Jon Smith, by the way," said Chris extending his hand. "But around here I'd be known as Chris."

Dare wiped his hands on his shorts and shook his hand. "I'm Dare Davis. But to be honest, sir, I know who you are. I know JoBell Leonard real well. We grew up together during the summers here. She told me your name after I told her about the visit you paid to Rob Wingate the other night. I was here listening to the band."

"Ah, that," said Chris. "That was some unfinished business from a long time ago. Jo and I had a rather unusual first meeting but perhaps she told you about that as well. It's all a very difficult and shocking situation. Pretty hard to wrap my head around. That's why I came down here. Took a bit of a lunch break from the roofing business to try to think about other things. So, if you don't mind, can we stick to talking about boats?"

"No problem, Chris," said Dare. He really had no desire to get caught in the middle of all of Jo's family uproar, and he suspected an uproar it must have been as she hadn't texted him since their beach walk. But they sometimes went several days without communicating when they were both really busy, so he knew sooner or later he'd get the full story.

"Would you like to come on board and take a look around?" Dare said. "I love showing her off. Jeff might be stopping by, and I imagine you'd enjoy meeting him too since you knew his uncle so well."

"Would love to," said Chris, and he stepped quickly on board. "Feels like home to me. Wow, this is one incredible piece of work."

For the next half hour, Dare and Chris discussed every aspect of the boat. Their mutual love and respect for fishing and for fine fishing vessels was evident, and Chris was suitably impressed with Dare's knowledge and his passion.

"Ever think of becoming a captain yourself? Chris asked as they stepped back onto the dock.

"It's my goal," Dare said excitedly. "I am really getting close on hours now and I've saved up enough for the testing. Probably get it sometime this fall if all goes well, and honestly, I can't wait. Jeff and some of the others have been helpful in preparing me, but like they say, they can't take the test for me. I'll be ready."

"Do you have enough saved to buy a boat?" the older man asked.

"Ha!" laughed Dare. "I wish. That's somewhere down the line. But once you have your license, it's for life, so guess I'll just have to wait to hit the lottery."

Chris smiled. "Hope you do someday, Dare. You'll make a great captain. I'd really love to talk more about what all goes on here now. I'm sure it has changed since nineteen seventy-five. Have any time tonight?"

"Tonight would be the only night," said Dare. "Once we get started again, well, you know, it's early mornings and long days. By the time I get her ready for the next day, I'm beat." He shrugged. "But yeah, tonight would be fine. What are you thinking?"

"Well, I've only been here what, three days? But that Marcie makes a mean shrimp basket, so could we meet there at six?"

"It's a plan," said Dare. "Can I have your number in case anything comes up? I'll text you if it does, but right now that should work."

They exchanged numbers and Chris started back to the van. He was just about to climb in when he saw a car parked spaces away. He thought he recognized the driver, and he did. It was Mike Leonard.

"Fancy meeting you here," said Mike as he got of the car. "Small island."

"Yeah, small island for sure," said Chris walking over. "Did my guys get started on the roof?"

"They did," said Mike. "And since I know nothing about roofing, I can't tell you how they're doing but I do know they're hard at it."

"Good," said Chris. "They'd better be because I've got job requests coming through the roof, pun intended."

Mike laughed. "Well, I guess that's a good problem to have. I'm going to enjoy a nice lunch here on the docks. I'm sure we'll cross paths again at this rate."

"Probably," nodded Chris. "Any, um, news for me?"

Mike thought for a moment before he responded. "Well, SeaAnna and Susan both know you're on the island. It was a very difficult conversation, as you can imagine. I don't know that either one of them is ready to have contact with you yet. My wife has agreed to the DNA testing. I think for her that's a first step and she won't do anything else unless and until she knows the answer from that. And Susan... Chris, I can't tell what she's thinking. She pretty much left the room where we were talking and I don't know anything more. I do know SeaAnna is there with her now, but they have their own issues to work through. Jo is out enjoying some beach time and I think she wanted to have some time to herself."

"Yeah, that's probably a good thing. We all need time," said Chris. "That's why I took my lunch break down here. This place holds a lot of great memories for me. Some things are very different, from what I can see. It's been a lot of years. But the beauty of the boats and the hold they have on me I guess have never changed. I sure felt it walking along there. I'd forgotten how much I enjoyed my time as a mate. I spent a little time with Jo's friend, Dare. Nice kid. Sharp too. Hope he succeeds."

"He is a good guy," Mike agreed. "Well, I will catch you later, Chris. We're leaving in the morning before the maddening crowd arrives. If anything changes with SeaAnna, I'll let you know but don't hold your breath. She's pretty stubborn."

"Got it," said Chris. "Take it easy, Mike, and thanks. This has put you in an awkward position. Maybe we'll see each other again sometime?"

Mike said nothing but nodded.

Chris got in his work van and headed out. Mike watched him go and wondered where all this was heading. Then his stomach rumbled and he decided to head over to the Tides Restaurant. It was a bit ramshackle but the seafood was fresh and the ambiance at the dock couldn't be beat. He had always enjoyed watching the activity there. SeaAnna and Jo didn't realize that in a way he enjoyed his time on the island. It was just always fraught with so much drama. Maybe things would be better now. Maybe. He ordered some fish bites, fries, and a beer, knowing SeaAnna would completely disapprove. But for the first time that day, he relaxed. He watched the pelicans on their perches and heard the gulls squawking and squabbling about something. And he tried to think about nothing at all.

He spent the better part of two hours just sitting, then he decided to walk around and see how storm repairs were coming along there. He was amazed at how quickly things seemed to go back to normal, but here and there were the tell-tale signs of damage. He'd noticed on the drive down the large piles of debris that had accumulated on the sides of the highway, so he knew there had been a lot of flooding people couldn't see. *Storms are like that*, he mused. *They can devastate one area or neighborhood and just a few miles away it's like nothing happened.* Tornadoes, hurricanes, severe thunderstorms – they all acted that way. Fickle. But if the island was anything, it was resilient, and that resilience was very evident at the docks.

He looked for Dare on the *Carefree* but didn't see him and suspected he had gone somewhere for a late lunch break. Other mates were still working, getting their boats ready for a strong shoulder season. He stopped and chatted with a few of them. The general consensus was that while Hurricane Eva had been rough, the damage could have been worse, and by and large they felt ready to get back to work. There were no guarantees there wouldn't be another storm, so they wanted to work as much as they could. Mike reflected that his work as a successful accountant couldn't be more different from what those folks did, but he enjoyed what he did, even if seeing their tanned and toned bodies made him feel his age a bit more. He laughed to himself and took a very long and leisurely drive back to the motel. He could see Jo out on the sand and she looked to be sound asleep. He decided a nap would be a great idea so he walked into the room, stretched out on the bed, and promptly fell asleep.

When he awoke, he realized he had slept quite some time. He opened the door to look out on the beach but Jo was nowhere in sight. Then he glanced at the room clock – 4:30. He took out his phone and checked for messages but nothing from SeaAnna. He took that as a good sign. Hopefully, she and Susan were trying to work things out between them.

For her part, Jo had had a refreshing day which, once upon a time, would have been all she asked for – a quiet day to herself on the beach. But today, her thoughts were continually invaded by Chris, and how she felt about him. Did she feel anything? How could she? She didn't even know the man. And she didn't know if he would reciprocate her feelings in any way. She roused herself at about a quarter after four, went for a quick dip in the ocean, and headed back to the motel office. She'd just have enough time to catch up with Lauren and make certain they were ready for tomorrow, jump into the shower behind the office, and then redress and wait for her dad for dinner. A day at the beach always made her very hungry, so the idea of a quiet meal with her dad and some good seafood was very satisfying.

"Hey Lauren, how's it been going?" she asked as she entered the office.

Lauren looked up. "I swear everyone in four states wants to come and see us if not tomorrow or this weekend, then sometime before Thanksgiving. I have never been so busy. But I'll tell you one thing. The day has flown by." She smiled. "However, everything's ready and all the staff is ready too. Oooh – look at you! Boy, did you get sun!"

Jo walked into the office bathroom and looked in the

mirror. Her face was tan but the extra layer of sun today had given it that sun-kissed look. Her shoulders had a layer of pink on them as well. She was glad she remembered to turn over at some point or she really could have been burnt.

"You'd think for someone who lives at the beach, I wouldn't burn at all," laughed Jo. "But I'll be stuck in classes soon enough and this will all fade. I'm going to hop in the shower and get dressed and then we'll go over a few more things before Dad picks me up at six."

"Fine," said Lauren but the phone was already ringing again so she left her to it, and got ready for dinner.

Mike, as punctual as ever, walked in to the office at six. He introduced himself to Lauren and thanked her for filling in.

"No problem, Mr. Leonard," she said. "This is a great place to work. I hope Miss Susan will keep me on once Jo is gone during the off-season. I heard she took a fall during the storm. Is she coming along?"

"It would take more than a hurricane to stop Susan," Mike chuckled. "Thanks for asking. She's walking pretty well and I expect you'll see her in a few days. She's about to bust a gut to get over here."

"Hey Dad," said Jo. "Hope you had a nice afternoon. Is Mom still with Gran?"

Mike checked his phone yet again although he knew he hadn't received anything. "As far as I know, yes. Haven't heard anything at all, so I'm taking no news as good news. Are you ready?"

Jo nodded and asked Lauren once more if she needed anything more and if she was OK with closing.

"It's all good, Jo, really. Now go on and enjoy Marcie's. I'll just dream about her shrimp baskets while you're gone.

Call me or text me tomorrow and let me know the schedule for the next week since we're back in operation."

"Will do," Jo called over her shoulder as she and Mike made their way to the car. "Good day, Dad?" she asked again.

"Yes, it was. I spent time at the docks, ran into Chris, didn't see Dare, ate too much lunch, and took a nap. What more could a guy ask for?"

"You saw Chris? How was he?"

"He seemed OK to me, although I know he is still processing all of this. He was surprised that your mom agreed to the testing, but I think he understands she just wants to set the record straight. Apparently, he and Dare had a great chat just before I got there. The two of them hit it off from what I gather, but remember, Chris was a mate too."

"Hadn't really thought of that," said Jo. "But I wonder if Dare knew who he was?"

"They seemed to have figured that out because he said he met Dare, your friend," said Mike.

"Knowing Dare, he was probably totally up front with him. That's just his way. Open and honest. He's always been that way. It's one of the things I like about him."

"Mmm," was all Mike said as they pulled into Marcie's. "Isn't that Dare's car there?"

"It is," said Jo. She realized they hadn't texted or talked to one another since yesterday morning. "Would you mind if we all sat together?"

"Not at all," said Mike as he opened the door to the restaurant. He saw Jo hesitate and take a step backward. "Are you OK? What's wrong?"

Jo gestured to where Dare was sitting, but he wasn't alone. Chris was there and they appeared deep in conversation. Just as Jo turned to tell her dad maybe they should leave, Dare spotted her and waved. "Jo, Mr. Leonard, come on over."

Mike looked at Jo. She shrugged as if to say, "My life gets crazier by the moment," and walked to the table.

"Hey Dare, and hello Chris," she said. "Didn't expect to see you here."

"Small island," said Mike again looking at Chris. Chris chuckled. "Dare and I found we had a lot in common during our brief conversation at the docks today, so we decided to continue it over dinner. Dare says after tomorrow, he will be one busy mate, and I get that totally." He suddenly sensed Jo's discomfort and realized he had momentarily forgotten the reality of the situation. "Hey look, if you three want to spend some time together, it's fine. I'm OK with leaving. But if you're OK with me being here, this is a table for four and you're welcome to join us."

They all looked at Jo who took a deep breath and said, "I won't get to see much of Dare either after tonight and Dad leaves in the morning and, Chris, well, we maybe can have a civil conversation this time." Then she grinned. "Sure, it's fine."

Marcie had been watching the interaction from behind the bar and had no idea what the connections were with the man named Chris, but Jo seemed OK with everything tonight, so she accepted that. "MaryAnn, run over there and get their orders," she said. "I know Jo is lemonade but I don't know about the others."

The infamous shrimp baskets and beers were ordered, and the conversation remained centered around boats and fishing. Mike didn't contribute much but he enjoyed seeing the younger man's passion. Chris, to his credit, was a good listener. Jo watched Chris intently, trying to sort out her feelings. She finally sat back and realized that she liked the man, grandfather or not. She could have dinner and let it go from there. She wasn't going to push but she wasn't going to ignore him either. She didn't agree with her mom and grandmother, but as Dare and her dad both had said, to each his – or her – own. Chris seemed happy enough to see her.

The baskets had been cleared away when Dare looked around and said, "This has been a lot of fun and, Chris, it's been a pleasure. Don't be a stranger at the docks. I've got a very early morning, so I'm heading off. Here's my part of the bill," and he handed Chris some cash. "Nope, my treat tonight, Dare. Save your money for that boat of your dreams."

Dare thanked him and came around to give Jo a hug. She knew he was leaving to give her, Dad, and Chris some time to talk, and she realized she appreciated that. "Good luck tomorrow, you," she smiled. "I know you'll be flat out tomorrow night but let me know how the day goes."

"Will do. Thanks again, Chris, and Mr. Leonard, hope to see you back on the island again sometime soon." As he made for the door, Mike suddenly jumped up and said, "Hold on, Dare, I need to talk to you about something."

Even Chris saw through that ruse, and as Mike and Dare disappeared outside, he looked over at Jo. She was sitting with an expression of mild amusement. "Well, here we are," she said. "I promise, no fainting this time."

"Glad to hear it," said Chris. "Look, Jo, I do appreciate your honesty with me the other night. Hell, if I hadn't heard it from you, I would have eventually heard it from someone else but without knowing Susan's side of the story. I understand from your dad that your mom and grandmother have spent the day together. Do you think either one of them will want to meet me? I know it's going to be really strange, but honestly, I would love to see Susan again. And I don't know your mom, but knowing you, I'm sure she's a wonderful woman."

"They both are," said Jo. "But Gran took it really hard about the testing. She feels like you think there was someone else, you know, after you left. It's like you don't believe her and that hurt her more than you showing up here again, I think."

Chris sat silently for a moment. "It's not that I don't believe her, Jo. I do. But before we all rush headlong into creating a new family dynamic, isn't it best to have no doubts? I guess I shouldn't have pushed that issue now that I think of it. Really stupid on my part. I'd love to apologize."

Jo shook her head sadly. "I just don't know, Chris. I haven't spoken to her at all since we had dinner last night and this all blew up. She kind of locked herself in her room. I have no idea what she and Mom discussed today, but they had their own issues to work on and this just compounds it all. I wouldn't hold my breath waiting on a positive answer to your question."

Chris sat back. "I don't know what to say, but as I told your dad earlier, I guess we all need to wait. Time has a way of working things out for us, even if we can't see it right now. I would like for you and me to keep in touch if that's OK. You know, texting, I guess. That seems to be the MO these days."

"Well, I'll be here probably for another ten days or so before I head back to Wilmington. We can meet here for a meal now and then, that's probably better than at the motel because Gran will be up and about really soon and she'll definitely be at the office."

Out of the corner of his eye, Chris caught Mike returning. "That's fine, Jo. Thanks for being a good sport and joining us this evening. By the way, Dare is one bright fellow. I have no doubt he'll get that captain's license. Does he have the means to get a boat? He kind of told me that was not in the cards."

Again, Jo shook her head. "Dare's family gets by, but that's about it. They all work hard but I doubt there's a big nest egg hidden away somewhere. But he'll save and even if it's a skiff, he'll get a boat someday."

Mike had arrived at the table. "Hate to break this up, but SeaAnna just texted me and she's ready to go back to the motel."

"Any idea ....?" Jo began.

"None," said Mike. "But I'll find out shortly. Jo, I probably need to get you home. You've got a full day tomorrow and I expect you've got work lined up too, Chris."

Chris motioned to Marcie for the check and indicated to Mike and Jo the dinners were on him. He stood and shook Mike's hand. "Hope to see you again sometime, Mike. Have a safe trip back."

"Best to you as well, Chris," Mike said.

Jo hesitated and then shook Chris's hand as well. "We'll keep in touch." Then she and Mike waved to Marcie and walked out.

The clear night air had a bit of a chill. Jo looked up and saw the Milky Way. It always took her breath away.

"Dad, do you think we'll get this worked out?"

"Jo, it's going to work out one way or the other. I think you and Chris at least have the ability to converse and that's a good starting place. Can't speak for the others. You know that."

They drove in silence and SeaAnna was waiting for them at the bottom of the steps when they got to the house.

Jo got out and left the door open for her. "Did you and Gran have a good day?"

"Actually, yes, we did," said SeaAnna yawning. "Our conversation earlier today on the beach helped me talk to her in a way I haven't for years. Who knows, maybe ever? We broke down some walls and talked honestly and I think we're on our way to healing. A lot of this was my fault, so I have to own that. We really tried to focus on us as mother-daughter and didn't talk much about Chris. I don't think she wants to talk to him any time soon. But I thought I heard in what she said today some possibility she could change her mind. And as you know, I'm going to wait. It might be the wrong thing to do but that's my choice."

She hugged Jo and got into the car. "We'll see you in the morning before we go. Try to get a good night's sleep. I love you, Jo."

"I love you both. See you in the morning," she said and she waved as they drove off. She knew they couldn't see her but she stood there for a long time thinking about the hug her mom had given her and how good it felt. She hoped that Gran would be as forgiving. After all, it was Jo who brought Chris back into her life, and clearly, he was not welcome.

"Gran," she said softly as she entered the house. It was dark inside.

"I'm here, Jo, laying on the couch. I turned off all the lights when your mother left. I just wanted to lay here and look at the stars through the window. Sorry, I forgot you'd be coming home too. It's gorgeous out there tonight."

"Yeah, it is," said Jo, sitting down on the edge of the couch. "I saw them earlier and the Milky Way always captivates me. But, Gran, are you OK? You and Mom, I mean. Better?"

"Yes, sweetie, better. We should have had the conversation we had today a very long time ago. But maybe that old saying better later then never is true. We still have, as you say, work to do, but I think some of her old resentment is gone and I need to keep from pressing buttons. I'm pretty good at that, you know?"

Jo smiled in the darkness and then yawned. So much had happened in just one day. She had set things in motion but now the end results were out of her control.

"Gran," Jo began.

"Jo," Susan said. "I know what you're going to ask me. Don't push, Jo. The answer is probably no, but I keep thinking. I'm thinking and thinking. I'll let you know when and if I have an answer for you."

Jo hugged her and said "That's good, Gran. I'm off to bed. If I don't see you in the morning, I will call around lunchtime. We are nearly full, so it's going to be crazy. Rest well."

Jo walked down the hallway to her room. She pulled back the curtains knowing the first light would wake her. But she also wanted to look out and see the stars. She got into bed and saw a glimpse of Orion, her favorite constellation, and then she fell into a deep and satisfying sleep.

Chapter Ten

Jo tried to be as quiet as possible but Susan had been up for hours after a night tossing and turning, so the little noises Jo made while tiptoeing across the floor and removing her yogurt from the refrigerator didn't bother her. What was bothering her was Chris. There were times during the night she could almost feel him next to her, holding her, loving her in a way that she had never experienced before or since. She knew that despite her best efforts over the years, she had never really forgotten him, or the way he made her feel. But she also knew he'd left her. Whether or not the story he told Jo was true, he also doubted her. That was the worst part. It made her sick to her stomach. There was a sadness that she just couldn't seem to overcome. It was all-encompassing, and even with the beautiful sunshine streaming through the windows indicating yet another "Chamber of Commerce" day, she felt gloomy and overwhelmed.

She swung her feet over the edge of the bed and took a deep breath. No, at the moment, she didn't know exactly what she'd do about Chris. But she did know what to do about something else that was bothering her. She'd get out of the house today, get some fresh air, and see what the island looked like roughly ten days after the storm. Since it was her left ankle she'd hurt, she had no qualms about driving. It was still a bit sore but not swollen, so she'd have to be extra careful going up and down the steps. She could, if needed, go one step at a time. She hadn't said anything to Jo about wanting to get out. Jo would likely have coddled her a bit more, and while she appreciated that, she also knew she had been cooped up in the house for too long.

She showered with a new sense of purpose and decided that she'd moped enough. Time to get back to the real world and make an appearance. Now that her neighbors had retrieved her car from its safe haven at the airport, she'd take a quick road tour of the island and then stop at the Sunshine Mart to pick up some groceries. She'd be back before Jo called to check in at lunch. She washed her hair and decided to let it air dry. It was short enough that when the wind caught the little bit of curl she had she thought it almost looked good enough for a fashion magazine. She laughed at herself, finished getting dressed, made a quick list for the grocery store, and then carefully made her way down to the car. Susan had always told Jo if she wanted to use it during the summer, she could, but Jo preferred to take the bike. That gave Susan the chance to come and go as she pleased and, in the end, that had worked out well for both of them.

Susan took her time driving through the villages. She knew some of the back roads that the tourists rarely, if ever, drove on. She saw the flooding devastation and too many houses to count with windows and doors wide open, in an effort to try to dry things out and combat the mold that grew insidiously in the days following a tropical system. She saw the CERT trailer in full operation and decided that if they still needed volunteers, she'd try to help out in the next few days before Jo headed back to university. That thought gave her pause and she unexpectedly felt a lump form in her throat. She loved having Jo with her in the summers, and this year, Jo had really been a tremendous help at the motel. She pretty much handled things on her own and that had been a boon to Susan who found herself starting to dread the annual summer grind. She'd done it for so many years she was afraid she'd lost track of herself. She'd never known another life. She was thrilled Jo had followed in her footsteps with her interest in jellyfish. She was proud of her and she would miss her terribly. There was another reason to get out of her funk. She wanted these last few days with Jo on the island to be happy ones.

She drove by the docks, which were bustling with activity. With the good weather and visitors coming back, the charter business would be in full throttle. She was impressed by the repairs she noticed, and thought that on the whole, the island had fared better than it could have. Small consolation, she knew, for the people whose homes were flooded, but life was almost back to normal and she was grateful.

She parked for a while, opened her windows, and just

enjoyed the view, the salt air, and the gentle breeze. She was lucky to have been born and raised in such a wonderful environment. The island could have its moments but it was truly the paradise most visitors thought it was. Hundreds, if not thousands, of guests had mentioned to her they hoped to retire on the island. Some of them did. Happily, not all of them, as it would be even more crowded than it was now. So many changes over the decades. She'd like to think she was still the same Susan but she wasn't that naïve. It was also a tough life when you had to make a living here. The years had given her a certain kind of "street smarts" – maybe "island smarts" was a better term. Her circumstances had knocked the stars out of her eyes at a pretty young age. She was thankful she'd lived long enough to put that all in the rearview mirror and enjoy just living here. Ah, but then Chris had to come back into the picture.

Her revery interrupted by that thought, she drove on to the grocery store. As she got out of the car, she could hear voices coming from somewhere on the top of the roof and assumed that the Sunshine Mart was having some repair work done. She'd seen plenty of contractors hard at work on her drive. She entered the store, grabbed a cart, and had several brief but enjoyable conversations with folks she hadn't seen in several weeks. She made sure to get the kind of yogurt that Jo liked, one with probiotics. Susan herself didn't care for yogurt, but Jo did. As she placed the carton in the cart, she again thought of how lonely she'd be with Jo back at school. She selected a bottle of wine for the evening. Hopefully, they'd have some time over the next few days just to relax in the evenings and kind of put the whole summer in perspective.

She had loaded her car, returned the cart, and was just about to start the car when she noticed Ray, the owner of the store come around the corner from the rear. He was deep in conversation with someone. With a gasp, Susan realized Ray was speaking to Chris. After all the years, she knew it was him before she could actually see him clearly. His build, albeit a bit heavier now, was the same, and the bits of gray around his sandy hair made him even more handsome. He was tanned apparently from the work he'd been doing lately. It was only then that Susan noticed the burgundy-colored JCS Roofing van parked at the far end of the lot. She felt her heart beating faster and her throat was dry. It looked like the two men might be wrapping up their conversation. She saw them nodding and shaking hands. There was no way she wanted him to see her, although she realized on a sunny day looking into an unfamiliar car – if he even noticed it – he'd be unlikely to recognize her. She was taking no chances. She saw no traffic oncoming so deliberately went out the entrance way and headed directly home.

She unloaded the bags making several trips, taking one step at a time as she'd promised herself. With every trip, her determination became stronger. By the time she'd taken everything upstairs and put the items away, she'd made up her mind. It was too early yet for wine, but a cold iced tea would be perfect. She sat on the couch and waited for Jo to call as she knew she would. Sure enough, right before noon, the phone rang. She took a deep breath and tried to sound steadier than she felt.

"Hi, Jo, love. How are things?"

"Good, really good. Mom and Dad came by as they promised and they are well on their way. Should be pretty close to home by now. It was great for Mom and me to part ways actually being OK with one another. I owe you that, Gran."

"Well, I owe you because your mom and I had some of the best discussions we've had in years. I think things may be on the mend there too and I'm happy for that. We had a lot of fences to mend. I'm glad we didn't wait too long. Time passes way too quickly and things need to be settled." Susan sighed and Jo heard it.

"Gran, are you OK? What have you done with yourself this fine morning?"

"Now, don't throw a hissy on me, but I took the car out, drove around, got some groceries, and am safely home. I even got your yogurt."

Jo thought briefly about saying something but decided against it. Her grandmother was perfectly capable of making decisions and doing whatever she wanted to do. So, she said instead, "How did the ankle hold up?"

"Actually, fine. No worse for wear." Susan paused. "Um, listen, Jo. I need for you to do something for me. Now that I'm mobile, I need to see Chris. Today. I know he's working, so maybe like half past four? At the motel beach. Will you do that for me?"

Of all the favors Jo might have expected, that wasn't one of them. She was quiet for a few seconds before she responded. "Gran, I'll be happy to text him and see what he says. I'll get back to you. Are you sure you're ready to see him and all?"

"I've done my thinking and it's time he and I have a talk. I'm not ready to share any more than that, but some things just need to be done. Procrastination won't help me here."

"OK, then. I'll get back to you when I hear back. If you want to come by and see me beforehand..."

"No, I think I'll just park and go out to the beach. I bought some nice wine for us to have later tonight if you're not too late."

"Lauren will close tonight, so I'll have time, Gran. You know if you need me, I'm here. You'll still probably get home before I do."

"Yes, I think I will be. Look, thanks, Jo. I'd do it myself but you're the one with his number. And he knows you. At least you've spoken a few times."

"Sure, Gran, if that's what you want, I'll do it."

"Thank you. Bye, love," replied Susan.

"Bye, Gran. Love you." Jo put down her phone and stared at nothing for a few minutes. She knew Susan had told her last night she was thinking, but Jo didn't have any idea she'd actually want to see Chris so soon. What did this mean? Would they pick up where they left off? Start anew? There were too many possibilities to consider, so Jo took yet another page from Dare's book of tackling something head-on. She texted Chris. It wasn't even a minute before she got a reply.

Hey there. Your message took me by surprise. But of course I'll see her. I can certainly make 4:30. Thanks.

Jo wasn't sure if anything further was needed from her end, so she just waited a few minutes more and then texted Susan.

He'll be there, Gran. Love u.

Susan sat for a long time reading and re-reading Jo's message. It wasn't that it was hard to interpret. It was just that she was unsure about her own motives for wanting to meet Chris when not forty-eight hours before she had sworn she wouldn't. But as she said to Jo, some things just needed to be dealt with, and as they always say, there's no time like the present.

She tried to fix herself some lunch but her stomach wasn't cooperating. She paced the floor, tried to nap, and finally settled on playing endless games of solitaire on her phone while the time passed. At three thirty, she decided she'd wear a linen blouse and clean shorts and maybe put on just a little make up. She convinced herself she only wanted to look presentable. She wasn't trying to be the girl Chris knew. She wanted to be herself as an adult woman who had an important conversation ahead of her.

"You can do this," she said to herself as she looked in the mirror. "There's really no other option. You'll be fine. You've thought it through. You're going to be OK."

She made her way back down the steps and into the car. As she parked at the motel, the shadows were already lengthening in the afternoon sun, so she chose to sit closer to the water's edge rather than up next to the motel. Besides, there may be guests around and this had to be a very private conversation.

Jo had been looking for her grandmother's car. She saw her start to walk out onto the beach and then lost sight of her as she walked between the buildings. She thought about going out to talk to her but she immediately changed her mind when she saw Chris's work van pull in next to her grandmother's car. He took his time getting out, seemed to pause for a few seconds, and then walked slowly but determinedly out to see Susan.

Susan felt his presence before she actually saw him. She was sitting on a towel facing the ocean, looking to the soothing waves for inner peace and courage. He walked around to face her and she stood up.

"Susan. Oh my God. It's you. After all these years. You look wonderful. It's good to see you. How are you?"

"I'm fine," Susan replied with an edge to her voice. "Well, as fine as I can be, I suppose. I'm sure Jo told you about my ankle. That's pretty much all healed now. I wish some other things could heal as easily."

"Susan," Chris started again. "This has all been unbelievable. If it wasn't happening to me, I'd think it was a plot in some book or movie. I don't know where to start. I've hardly thought about anything else since I met Jo and we learned the truth. By the way, she's a wonderful young lady and I know you're proud. There's a lot of your spunk in her. And I'm sure SeaAnna is every bit that amazing. If I had only known." He shook his head. "If, if, if. That's all that I seem to come up with. Pretty weak, I know, but it's truth. All these years, I thought you'd just given up on me. I had my hands full. And time passed. We both know it was different then. Jo told me, and Mike too, about all you went through with SeaAnna and your parents." His eyes turned sad. "I loved you and I let you down. And I don't know what to say."

Susan looked at him and saw that wonderful boy/man that she had loved so much. For years, she'd hoped they'd somehow find each other again. Her heart ached and she wanted to just throw her arms around him and let him carry her away. But the reality was this man had also hurt her and she just couldn't let that go. "I have always dreamed of this day, Chris. You see, I really did love you. Maybe I still do. And I think I can almost let go of Rob Wingate and his stupidity and our lack of trying to get in touch over all those years. But for you to think, to infer, that somehow in the few weeks after you left the island I was off sleeping with every Tom, Dick, or Harry that came along like some kind of slut or tramp or whatever you want to call it, that's just unreal to me. To ask for a DNA test? Why? To embarrass me in front of my daughter and granddaughter? To question my integrity? It's more than I can bear, Chris."

Chris looked down and was quiet. "I know that asking for that test was a stupid thing to do, Susan. It all was on me so quickly, I just thought maybe it would give us all time to sort through our feelings and...and...."

"There are no 'ands' on this one, Chris." Susan had found her stride and now felt there was no holding back. "What made you come back here? Did you want to see what had become of me? Why? I just don't understand. You've made a fool out of me."

"Susan. Again. I thought you had no use for me. I assumed, if I thought it through, that you had finished school, were happily married and settled somewhere. I had no idea at all you'd still own the motel or that you'd even be here. I came because I heard about the storm, and I remembered how bad it was after Evelyn. I have a company now that's in a position to help and I have the time to help. That's all I wanted to do. And if I am completely honest, I missed this island. Coming here again brought back some really good memories for me, believe it or not. And when Jo texted me today, I thought maybe you'd want to try to see how we can move forward from this. I know it won't be easy but Jo and I seem to have made a good start."

He stepped forward to try to take her hand but Susan stepped back. "No, Chris. Jo is coming at this from a very different place. She never knew you. Now, all of a sudden, she has a grandfather she never knew she had. It's all very exciting for her. She can develop her feelings over time and as she sees fit. SeaAnna too. I knew you, Chris, and I loved you. And you've let me down before we even had a chance to get started."

Chris stepped back and his voice took on a hard edge. "So then, just why did you want me to come out here and have this chat?"

"To tell you I don't want any second chances. I don't want to see you. I don't want to speak to you. Ever. What kind of relationship you develop with Jo, or with SeaAnna if the test comes back with a linkage, and I can assure you it will, is up to you and up to them. But I am out of it. I've made it on my own all these years, and that's just how it will stay."

"I'm so sorry, Susan..."

But Susan cut him off. "As far as I'm concerned, we're through here. Enjoy your time on the island. And if our paths cross, you don't know me, OK? It would have been better if you'd never come back, Chris."

"Would it, Susan? I'm sure now that I have a daughter and granddaughter. Would it have been better for me never to know that? It was probably stupid, it *was* stupid, for me to ask about a DNA test. But I said I'm sorry and I really am. What else do you want me to do?"

"Please leave," said Susan. She was trying hard to hold back the tears and she didn't want Chris to see her crying. "Just go. Now."

Chris shook his head. He opened his mouth to say something more but he didn't trust his emotions or his voice either. He felt incredible sadness. Could he have handled this better? *Yes, you damn well you could have*, he told himself.

He realized he was more in love with the woman he was walking away from than he ever could have imagined. But she had been very clear. Chris kept walking and didn't look up until he got into his car and drove out of the motel parking lot. He brushed away a tear and wouldn't allow himself to look in the rearview mirror.

Jo was waiting on the porch for Lauren's arrival when she saw Chris leave. He never looked up, never looked over to the porch to see if she was there. Jo had a sinking feeling that something went very wrong. How that happened she couldn't know at the moment, but a few minutes later when she saw her Gran, limping slightly and clearly sobbing, her heart broke. Like Chris, her grandmother made no effort to come by the office, so Jo could only assume she'd find out more when she got home, if her grandmother was willing to talk.

It was only a few minutes later when Lauren pulled up. Jo gave her a very quick rundown of the things she needed to know for the evening, and then she was pedaling home. She didn't know what she should do or say, but she figured whatever Gran wanted to do was fine with her.

When she walked into the house she could see Susan sitting with her back to her on one of the couches, a glass of wine in her hand. She sounded composed but not at all like her Gran. Jo walked over and gave her a big hug.

"Oh Gran," she said. "What happened? Did he upset you? Did you argue?"

"Neither of those things. Jo, I realized over these last two days I loved Chris my entire life. What life could have been with him we will never know. But I also know that I can't love someone who apparently didn't trust me. And that's something I can't forgive. I just can't. So, we're through."

"What do you mean, through?"

"I mean, I told him I did not want to see or talk with him ever again. If he sees me on the island somewhere while he's still here working, he's to ignore me."

"But…"

"Jo, what you and your mom decide to do with respect to Chris is up to you. I won't interfere. But just don't think I'll be a part of it."

Jo slumped down in the opposite couch and took a sip of the glass of wine Susan had already poured for her. "That's not what I expected, Gran, but then, I shouldn't have had any expectations. It is your life, and I guess if this is what you need to do, I'll try to understand. But it makes me sad."

"It makes me sad too, Jo, but life is full of sadness. Lucky for us, we've had our share of good times too, lots of them. Just know that I love you, Jo. And I'm going to miss you so much."

And with that, Susan began to cry again, real sobs that brought Jo to tears too. She walked over and took Susan in her arms and held her. They sat there together, each lost in their own thoughts as the day started to turn to dusk.

Susan suddenly looked up. "I saw that the roof on the motel looked in fine shape. Did someone fix it?"

Jo paused a second too long before answering.

"Was it Chris?" Susan asked.

"It was," said Jo. "Well, it was his crew. Dad arranged it with him. He wouldn't let us pay. Said he'd made enough mistakes and this was a very small way of trying to make good."

Susan laughed but without humor. "Well, that's one thing he got right. He's certainly made enough mistakes." Susan got up from the couch. "I know it's early but I'm off to bed now, Jo. We'll have a better night tomorrow."

Jo finished her wine and reflected on what had happened that afternoon.

No, thought Jo. *This wasn't how this was supposed to end at all.*

Chapter Eleven

The email arrived shortly after Jo had opened the office for the morning. All the repairs at the university had been completed, and the administration felt that students should no longer have issues in their own communities along the coast, so classes were to begin in a week's time. For upper class students, there would only be a day of moving in. Schedules and all other pertinent information would be sent by e-mail.

At that moment, Jo felt very ambivalent about things. She was definitely ready to get back to classes. She missed the stimulation in the classroom and seeing her friends. She would be especially happy to reconnect with her roommate, Justyna. They had been friends for many years, having attended the same boarding school for middle and high school. Justyna was also from Raleigh but had family in Poland which was where she'd spent her summer. They'd have plenty to talk about when they got back together.

Jo sent her a quick text to ask her about her return plans, and then texted Dare to let him know she'd likely have to leave as soon as the weekend was over. Labor Day would be frantic, and Jo would not leave her grandmother in a lurch. She'd stay to work the office. She knew it would be a tight time frame but if her mom or dad could pick her up on Monday around noon, she could be back in Raleigh late that afternoon. It would take her just a few days to gather things together, load her own car which she had left in Raleigh for the summer, and head down to Wilmington. With luck, she'd get there Wednesday evening and have all day Thursday to settle back in before classes started on Friday. She wondered why they just didn't wait to begin the fall term that following Monday, but she realized having lost time due to the storm, every day they could get in was important.

She wondered if the later start would mean cutting out some of the breaks they normally would have. She had fully intended to come back and see Gran as much as possible. Maybe SeaAnna would actually be visiting more now, and that would relieve some of the burden from Jo. She felt they both needed to be somewhat available to help Susan through the fall and winter. Jo was pretty sure Susan would eventually get her old self back, but she wanted to be sure. The whole thing with Chris had clearly taken a toll on her spirit.

When her phone pinged back with a message from Dare, she was surprised. She expected him to be out on a charter, and there was no time to text on that job.

Dare: *Hate to think about you leaving. Our charter canceled for the day. Doing a make-up half day. Dinner?*

Jo: *OK. Make it later – I want to spend some time with Gran after work. Lauren comes at 5.*

Dare: *7 ok?*

Jo: *7 is good. Rest of this weekend is slammed so this is it.*

He added a sad face emoji. Jo would surely miss him too. Dare was truly her best friend. She was glad for his cancellation, otherwise they might not have been able to connect in person for any length of time at all. She was absolutely going to spend her free time with Susan over the weekend, what little time there was. It was great to have Lauren to take the night shifts.

She called rather than texted Susan at lunchtime. She needed to hear her voice and make certain she was doing OK.

"I'm alright, I suppose. Just taking care of things around the house. Thought I'd go for a walk later, maybe on the new walking trail they put in the village. I think my ankle can handle it now. And I won't push it."

"I'll be by after work. Lauren is working from five until close tonight and for the weekend. And, Gran, I'll be heading back to school. Got the official word this morning. Need to get home Monday. I'll check to see if Mom or Dad will come to get me. Dare and I will have dinner tonight around seven so that gives you and me some time together after I get off. Then I'll be with you in the evenings through the weekend. OK?"

"That's fine, Jo. I'll need to come into the office and reacquaint myself with some things since I'll start working days again on Tuesday. How about I fix us some appetizers this evening before you go to see Dare? And if you're going to Marcie's..."

"I will bring you back a shrimp basket," Jo laughed. "I don't think we'll be late as he has another charter first thing tomorrow. Make me some of those stuffed mushroom things, please. See you later."

As Jo ended the call, she realized she had said that either Mom or Dad might pick her up. For years it had always been her dad, but maybe this time SeaAnna would come. At any rate, home was the next call on the list. And so, the afternoon was spent making arrangements for Monday (she was delighted to hear that it would be her mom coming to retrieve her), texting back and forth with Justyna, and making lists of the things she'd need to buy and the things she didn't want to forget to pack.

Between doing those things and taking care of business, it seemed like no time that Lauren was walking through the door.

"Lauren, I'll be leaving Monday afternoon," Jo told her as they finished going over the check-in list for the evening. "I think Gran is hoping you'll continue with the evenings, at least through September."

"I'm pretty sure it will work. We really need the money, Tim and me, so tell her I'll be available."

"Great. And thanks again, Lauren. You're a lifesaver."

Jo pedaled off, and before she knew it, she was showered and ensconced on a couch eating her grandmother's delicious mushroom bites along with some cheese and crackers.

"I think I'm part mouse," laughed Jo. "You won't be buying nearly as much cheese when I'm gone."

Susan smiled sadly. "I'd rather have you and the cheese around the house. It's just so hard to believe how the summer has flown by. This summer and all the summers. I remember when I brought you here the first time. I think you were five. Every little thing on the beach fascinated you and we spent hours arranging your 'findings' on the porch railing. That first year, it was the purple shell pieces. The next year, I think it was the huge scallop shells. Then whelks, scotch bonnets, and coquinas. But that year we had the big jellyfish show up on the beach, there must have been tons of them, you were beside yourself. Do you remember?"

"I do. And I remember you telling me there was so much to learn from them. And that you hoped one day I would study them so that I could share all their secrets with you." Jo sighed. She knew how much she'd miss her grandmother. " So, you know I have to go, Gran, as much as I'd love to stay. I'm not sure how much break time I'll have this fall but you know I'll pop back when I can. We can always video chat. And maybe Mom will drive over. Who knows?"

Susan actually broke into a grin. "She wanted me to keep this a secret but... She's driving here Sunday so she and I can spend some time together. Then the three of us can eat dinner Sunday night before you finish up at the motel Monday and go home."

"That's great, Gran. I am so happy that with everything else this summer brought, it brought the three of us to our senses and closer together. It feels good, doesn't it?"

"Indeed," nodded Susan. "Shouldn't you be heading off? Are you hiking to Marcie's or do you want to drive?"

"Neither. Dare texted me just as I was getting out of the

shower. He'll pick me up, so I imagine he'll be here soon. He's never late."

No sooner had Jo said that, she heard the crunch of the gravel in their driveway.

"See you, Gran. I won't be late. We both have to work in the morning. I won't forget to bring you that shrimp."

Jo hopped off the couch and headed down the steps. She was thankful that she and Dare would have one last night together before she headed off, even if it was only a quick bite at Marcie's.

The place was humming with the Labor Day crowd, so they felt lucky to find a spot at the bar. Marcie brought Jo her lemonade and Dare a beer. She took their orders but didn't have much time for small talk. Jo was glad to see how business had picked back up so quickly.

"I've got a lot to fill you in on, Dare," Jo said. "It's been a crazy couple of days. Some good things and some things I'm not so sure about. But I have taken your advice so many times recently just to tackle things head on."

"And?" Dare asked.

"Mixed bag, I think. But you decide."

Jo began to tell Dare about her mom and her grand-mother, her mom and her, and her grandmother and Chris. Their orders arrived, so a lot of the talking was interrupted with eating, with Dare nodding or shaking his head as the stories unfolded.

"You fit a lifetime of drama into a few days, Jo. But it's great that you and your mom seem to have come to an understanding, and your mom and grandmother as well. I don't know what to say about her and Chris. That's a tough situation to be in and I'm in no position to judge." He shrugged. "Maybe time will change things and maybe not. I have to say I like Chris a lot. He really knows his stuff about boats and all. He's already given me some great information that I think will be useful as I get ready for my exam. He's come around the docks a good bit when he can. Like I said, I like him."

They talked a bit more - about the Labor Day crowds, what fish he expected to be biting, what classes Jo would be taking, and his excitement about working toward his captain's license. When they finished, Jo gave Marcie a big hug and collected the take-out order for her grandmother.

"Dinner's on me tonight, kids," Marcie smiled. "You've been great customers all summer. Good luck back at school, Jo. Don't be a stranger when you come back during breaks."

"I won't be, Marcie. And you keep an eye on Gran for me. She's driving now and walking well, so she'll be here in person pretty soon."

"Good news," said Marcie. "Gotta run. The crowd is still coming in."

Dare and Jo got in the car and Dare asked if she'd like to just drive to one of the ramp lots to walk out onto the beach and see the stars just for a few minutes. Jo nodded. It was still early and they'd likely only be gone a few minutes. She had the take-out to deliver and there was nothing worse in Jo's mind than cold shrimp and fries.

"Just for a minute or two," Jo said. "You know I have precious cargo here."

Dare laughed. They drove just a few minutes north to where the wind surfers usually gathered at the place known as Canadian Hole, and caught the end of the sunset. The planets and stars were just beginning to pop out, twinkling brightly on the darkening sky. There was just a sliver of a moon.

They sat in companionable silence for a minute or two

and then Dare leaned over to kiss Jo. Not a peck on the cheek but a full-blown kiss. Jo stiffened and sat back a bit.

"Please, Dare. No. Let's not go there," she whispered.

"What?" he asked, his voice rising just a bit. There were plenty of other cars around and he didn't want to make a scene.

"Dare, you and I have been friends forever. You're like a rock to me. What we have is really special and I don't want that to change. We don't need to take our relationship into a place where we really can't fulfill it. You're here and I'm away at school and we need to focus on those things. Be each other's support system. I'm so sorry if you thought I wanted to be more than friends."

"But I thought you expected me to try something. That you'd think I didn't care if I didn't come on to you. It didn't feel right to me but since you're leaving…"

"You thought I expected that? That's, well, it seems like that's what society wants us to think. But no, I love our friendship, and in that way, I love you. I only expected you to be there for me like you've always have been. Please don't be upset. I can't take much more." Jo started to cry quietly.

Dare said nothing for a moment or two. He was thinking. Then he put his arm around Jo. When she flinched a bit, he said, "I'm just hugging you, Jo. And as hard as it is for you to believe, I'm OK with what you said. I love our friendship too. Like I said, I just didn't want you to think I didn't care."

"Caring is so much more than getting involved in a romantic relationship. Just be you, Dare. That's what is so awesome about you. I never have felt you didn't care. Your advice sometimes pisses me off, and you know we've had our moments, but I always know you care."

"So, we're good?" he asked.

"We're just fine, Dare." She smiled. "Now you'd better get me back home or there'll be hell to pay with this shrimp."

Dare gave her another quick hug and started the car. When they got to Susan's, he reached over and took her hand. "Thanks, Jo. And do well at school. I know you will. Text me. You know sometimes it takes me a while to answer but I will. And I'll see you during breaks, OK?"

"Absolutely." She kissed Dare lightly on the cheek. "You study hard as well. I can't wait to hear some good news later this fall." And with that she left, carrying the precious shrimp up to Susan.

Chapter Twelve

Time seemed to pass in a blur after that. Before Jo realized it, she was six weeks into the new term. She was enjoying her classes immensely, but then, she'd always enjoyed school. Dare was texting regularly. The charter business had continued to stay strong right into early October, so he hadn't had much time to study for his license testing, but things were starting to slow down just a bit. The weather cooled and vacationers were back home enjoying pumpkin spice lattes and vanilla candles. Jo could definitely sense the change of seasons.

SeaAnna and Jo talked every weekend. SeaAnna seemed to be more interested in what Jo was doing, and Jo tried her best to understand the intricacies of her mom's dabbling in real estate.

She also told Jo she had sent in her DNA sample to the testing company weeks ago, so an answer would likely be forthcoming. Thinking about that always made Jo's heart beat a bit faster. While she knew the outcome would be positive, she was still uncertain as to how SeaAnna would handle it moving forward.

Chris kept in touch once in a while through text messages. Their relationship was moving ahead slowly, but Jo sensed it was getting a bit stronger and deeper over time. Chris expressed a real interest in jellyfish as he had seen so many during his time as a mate, and the "pulsating blobs" as he called them were a fascination to him. Jo was pretty certain her professors wouldn't approve of that description, but nonetheless, at least Jo and Chris had found common ground.

Jo sensed he was spending a good bit of his free time at the docks with Dare. She knew they had even gone out a few times together with Jeff Neal on the *Carefree* on the odd day she wasn't booked or had had a cancellation. Chris would take photos of the jellyfish he saw floating along in the sound or in the open ocean, and Jo would identify them for him. Jo reckoned it was a good start.

It was a lovely fall afternoon and Jo and Justyna had a break between classes. Their differing schedules meant they didn't get to see one another often during the week. Their majors were different and sometimes they went for days without really having a chance to say more than good morning or good night.

On this day, they unexpectedly found themselves both

in their room at the same time, so they took the opportunity to catch up on things.

"What are you planning to do this weekend, Jo?" asked Justyna. "I'm headed home after classes Friday for my dad's birthday this weekend."

"I'm not sure," said Jo. "I miss not having a nice long fall break. I need to get up to Hatteras to see my Gran but it's a long trip for just two days."

"Did you see that poster for that upcoming concert on the quad? I think it's a group you mentioned to me before. A couple of names...um...Jason and the somethings?"

"You mean, Jamie and the Hanks?" exclaimed Jo. "No, I hadn't seen that. My friend Dare loves that group. I wonder if he'd be interested in coming down to hear them. Fishing season will really be pretty slow by then." She was excited. "I'll have to ask him. I don't know how I missed that."

"I just saw the posters being put up when I walked here from class," Justyna said. She was about to continue when suddenly Jo's phone pinged. It was a text from SeaAnna asking Jo to give her a call. Then it pinged again. Chris, same message. And then again from Susan.

"Whoa, what's going on?" Justyna asked.

"I think I might know," said Jo. "But I'll need to respond to all of this so I'm going to go outside and see what's up. See you later this evening." She stepped out of her dorm and found a nice bench under a tree where she could not just respond but also think. She decided to take them in the order in which she received them with SeaAnna's being first.

"Mom, is everything OK?" she asked when SeaAnna answered.

"Your dad and I are fine, so calm down. But I wanted

you to know the DNA testing results came back early this morning."

"And?" Jo felt her insides seize up.

"You were right. Chris is my biological father and you are his granddaughter."

Jo exhaled and started breathing again. "How do you feel? Are you OK? What are you going to do?" The questions tumbled from Jo.

"Over these last weeks, I really have come to expect this. When I was away from the island and could think rationally. Plus, your dad and I had several long talks. So I can't say I was truly surprised. But it's like falling over a waterfall. There are thoughts swirling all through my head and lots of emotions. I'm not sure where I'll land. But I did make one decision. Actually, I made it a few days ago. I decided that if the results came back positive, I would make plans to visit Chris personally. I can't call him Dad. Don't know if I ever will be able to. But I have to meet him and start to get to know him."

"And when are you going to do that?" interjected Jo.

"This weekend. I asked your dad for Chris's contact information and I texted him. Guess I beat him to the punch because he had received an email from Family Tree saying he had a significant familial match. And there I was."

"This weekend. Wow. Did he agree to meet?"

Jo expected she knew the answer. Chris would be her next call.

"He did. I'll stay with Mom Friday evening and he and I are meeting Saturday morning down at the docks. We can have coffee there and a bit of privacy if we sit on one of the benches along there. Shouldn't be too many people around this time of year."

"True," agreed Jo. "But what about Gran?"

"She was really happy when I called to say I was coming down. Not so happy when I told her why. She's still bitter about the whole testing thing. But I also sense she's been turning things over in her mind as well."

"So, you think she'll go with you?"

"No. Actually, I think this first meeting has to be for just Chris and me. And I'm not sure that for all her thinking, Mom is ready to meet with him. She may never, Jo. What was it you told me Dare said to you when you first told him? We all have to find our own way through this or something along those lines."

"I just wish it could be different," sighed Jo. "With Chris being there all the time you know they'll run into each other at some point."

"You'd think," agreed SeaAnna. "But apparently, that hasn't happened. I don't think Mom is getting out as much, which isn't good. But that whole issue will soon resolve itself."

"Why's that?"

"Chris said it was a good thing the DNA results came back when they did as he'll be leaving the island early next week. All the roofing work that he can do has apparently been done. He feels it's time to go back home."

"Wow." Jo found she didn't have anything to add. Then she asked, "Well, Mom, this is kind of exciting in a way. Is Dad going too?"

"No, just me. But we'll have a long talk when I get back and I'll fill you in if I can. I know this will be an emotional time."

"That's probably putting it mildly."

"I honestly don't know what I think or how I'll feel when the time comes. But it is exciting and terrifying for sure."

Jo looked at the time. If she was going to call both Chris and Susan before her next class, she'd need to end this call. But SeaAnna was already a step ahead of her.

"Jo, I've got to run. Thanks for calling me. Love you."

"Love you too, Mom. Bye."

Then she called Chris. Texting was usually their method of communication. Calling was another level of personal. But he asked her to. She first thought he wasn't going to answer and expected voice mail, but at the last second, she heard his voice.

"Jo, thanks for calling. I suspect you know, but your Mom is coming to the island this weekend."

"I know, Chris. She and I just spoke. Your texts came just about on top of one another. I figured it was about the test results. Wow. She just told me it's kind of exciting and terrifying at the same time. How are you feeling?"

"I'm very glad this is over. I keep hoping that now that this is going to be behind us, the test results I mean, that the passage of time will soften your grandmother's heart a little bit. Maybe she'll forgive me. And I can't wait to meet your mom. I mean, my daughter. It's surreal. But I told you before, if she's anything like you, and after all she raised you along with your dad who I like a lot, we'll be able to begin to work through this. I know it will be a process. It's kind of like what you and I are going through. A little bit at a time, eh?"

"That's right. I'll be on pins and needles this weekend but I think Mom is in a good place now. You're right about time. It helps. At least it did in this case. And thanks for sending all the jellyfish photos, by the way. It's actually good practice for me to try to ID them myself before actually looking them up. You've seen some amazing stuff."

"Yep. It's been fun to get to know Dare a bit more too,

141

when we go out on the *Carefree*. You know, he's really wound up about his testing, but honestly, I think he'll be fine. It's nerve-wracking in the run-up to the exams but I feel like he can do this."

"I do too. I'm proud of him," said Jo. "Hey, I hate to cut this short but I have a class coming up and there's one more call I need to make."

"Understood. I'll let you go. Thanks for calling, Jo. I'll keep in touch. Bye."

She ended the call with Chris and sat for a few moments before calling Susan. Obviously, Susan knew what was happening and had made her feelings pretty clear to SeaAnna. What should she say?

Maybe nothing at all. Just listen, Jo, she told herself. *Let Gran work through this on her own.*

Susan must have been waiting by her phone because she picked up on the first ring.

"Aw, Jo, I miss you. I guess you know why I'm calling. We got some news this morning. Can't say I'm surprised as I knew all along. Just some people didn't want to believe me."

She waited for Jo to respond and when Jo didn't, she continued. "I am looking forward to seeing your mom. This will be her second trip this fall. Can you believe it? We're moving toward normal. That makes me happy."

Jo relaxed. She wasn't prepared for a diatribe about Chris, so she was happy to change the subject. "Yes, she told me what fun you both had a few weeks ago. And she and I are talking regularly on weekends. It's been fun."

"It's a shame they cut out your fall break. It's been real pretty here. I'd been looking forward to seeing you."

"I know, Gran. But at least by the university doing this, we can keep our Christmas break intact. You know I'll see you then. Maybe Thanksgiving too. One way or the other, I'll see you. Either in Hatteras or in Raleigh."

"I hope it's here, Jo. I just don't feel like making that drive anymore."

"Well," Jo said. "We have plenty of time to discuss all of that. I'll see what Mom and Dad think, OK?"

"OK. But keep calling me. I love hearing from you and I'm so interested in your classes. Maybe I can get my degree just by learning from you."

Jo laughed. "You don't need a piece of paper, Gran. You're plenty smart. But I'll give you a degree from the University of Jo any time."

Susan laughed too. "I'm sure you have a class to go to or some studying or something, so I'll say goodbye. You always cheer me up. Love you, Jo."

"Love you too, Gran," and she ended the call. She wasn't sure how she'd keep busy over the weekend knowing what was happening. She decided to volunteer at Fort Fisher. They had a great jellyfish exhibit. Nothing better than spending time with pulsating blobs to keep your mind occupied. She laughed to herself and went on to class.

Chapter Thirteen

SeaAnna was quietly humming to herself as she drove down Highway 12. Normally, when Mike was driving, she would be looking at her phone and not really paying much attention to the scenery. But since she was driving today, she seemed to suddenly notice the wild beauty of the island. In the fall, it was so much quieter. The angle of the sun was softer, and the gold of the sea oats stood in contrast to the blue skies. There were clouds today, and the forecast for the weekend wasn't the best. But today was an enjoyable day for a drive on this national scenic by-way, and she wondered why she really hadn't paid it much attention before.

Of course, in her heart she knew why. She had always resented having to come back here. It never really felt like home to her. But if she was totally honest with herself, she never let it feel like home.

After she left for college, her visits home were brief and usually contentious. As years passed, Raleigh was where her friends were, where she and Mike built their home, and where they had made their life together.

Somehow, Hatteras seemed to fade into the background and she'd really made no effort to let it move from that spot. Even on the occasional visits to see Susan, she rarely took advantage of the beach or of any of the other beautiful areas on the island. She would "do her duty" as she sometimes put it to Mike, and then quickly return to where she felt more comfortable and accepted. Mike never fully under-stood her feelings, at least not until recently. Maybe now they could try to appreciate the island for what it was – a part of her history that was important and deserved a little better.

When she got closer to Susan's, her attention turned to the reason she was making this trip. She was going to meet her biological father. The enormity of this entire situation was not lost on her, but her feelings these past days had vacillated wildly. On some days, she was excited and happy. On other days, she felt unsure of herself and her emotions. She had promised herself, and Mike, that she would meet Chris with an open mind and wouldn't run head strong in any direction. Probably easier said than done, but she'd give it a try.

Obviously, she'd be staying with her mom, so Susan's thoughts and feelings would no doubt come into play. She'd hoped after meeting Chris, she and Susan could have a good heart to heart talk. She laughed to herself.

So often she'd heard of the crazy dynamics of other families and think how lucky she was. But now she realized she had ignored important issues in her own family. This weekend would be a time to continue the healing journey started this summer.

Things with Jo were going exceedingly well, and she found real happiness in that. Hopefully, she and her mom could continue their dialogue, and she and Chris would... would what? Start to get to know one another. That made sense to her as a first step.

She pulled into the driveway and saw Susan puttering with something on the porch railing. She was glad she'd left Raleigh around noon so that they'd have a bit of time this evening to relax. Tomorrow morning would come soon enough.

"So glad you're here," Susan called out as SeaAnna unloaded her overnight bag and headed up the stairs. "How was the drive?"

"Actually, it was OK," SeaAnna replied. "I don't think I ever really appreciated how this place looks in the fall. Everything seems to have a softer edge to it. It's kind of calming."

"It is, when the weather is nice. I'm glad you drove today because I think there will be some rain later tomorrow, and unfortunately, all day Sunday when you drive back. Wish you could stay longer. I've been kind of lonesome. With Jo's break erased, I really was happy to know you were coming again, although I'm not sure what tomorrow will bring for you. Are you sure this is what you want?"

"Yes, but let's leave that conversation for now, Mom. I

brought a few things to fix for supper tonight and a bottle of wine for us to share. Let's just enjoy that, shall we?"

Susan nodded her acquiescence and soon they were busy in the kitchen. Susan put on some light, soft classical music and they passed the evening talking about everything but Chris. Both of them were pleased with Jo's progress at UNCW, and Susan brought SeaAnna up to speed on all of the latest gossip on the island. It seemed no time at all before they were sitting in the dark, sunset coming earlier now. It was around nine that SeaAnna yawned.

"Mom, we could go on and on, I know. But it was a long drive for me, and I'd like to try to get a good night's sleep.

"What time is your, um, appointment tomorrow?" asked Susan trying to sound as disinterested as possible.

"We're meeting at the Tides for coffee around eight-thirty. We figured it would be relatively quiet then. What-ever boats are going out will be gone, and the rest are prob-ably done for the season. Will I see you in the morning?"

"I think I'll try to sleep in. I'll see you later in the day."

SeaAnna knew what her mother was doing by avoiding her prior to her leaving in the morning but she said nothing.

"OK, then," she said as she walked over to give Susan a small hug. "We'll talk later."

She went into the room that was normally Jo's during the summer. Bits and pieces of her daughter were still in existence in the room. There were photos, clippings, books, and even clothes. Susan just left the room that way, and SeaAnna realized that this place was a huge part of Jo's life. SeaAnna and Mike had helped make it that way in some regards by allowing her all those summers away, but she really believed Jo would have come to love this island no matter what, even if she'd never visited until she was eighteen.

It must be genetic, she's so much like her grandmother. Except, of course, with respect to Chris. Where would she, SeaAnna, fall on that scale? She had that one thought before she fell asleep.

When she opened her eyes, she was startled to realize she hadn't woken up at all during the night. *That hasn't happened in a long, long time,* she thought to herself. *Must be the salt air and my being tired. But I do feel refreshed.*

She showered and had a couple of pieces of toast just to settle the butterflies in her stomach. She wasn't trying to be noisy, just moving around normally, but Susan's door remained closed. She sat in quiet reflection until about a quarter after eight, then left the house, got into her car, and headed to the docks. She didn't want to seem too eager, but then, she didn't want to be late. That would be rude and there was no reason to go down that road. First impressions, after all.

She pulled into the lot at the Tides but didn't see the burgundy work van anywhere. It was twenty-five past the hour. She decided she could really use a coffee right then, so she walked into the restaurant to order. There, alone at a table facing the water, was a sandy and gray-haired gentleman who reminded her a bit of herself and of Jo. He heard her walk in and looked up.

"You must be SeaAnna." Chris stood up and beckoned her over to the table. He could see Jo in her and Susan too but maybe a bit of himself? He tried to be calm. "It is my pleasure to meet you. I mean, I am thrilled. I mean, please sit down. Wow. I guess I'm kind of nervous."

SeaAnna walked to the table with her heart racing. "I thought I'd gotten here first. I didn't see the van everyone's been telling me about. I had a speech all prepared for when you'd walk in, but now that's gone out the window. I'm guess I'm nervous too."

"The truck is in the shop. I thought I'd better have it checked out before I head back north. It's been through a lot these past few months. But that's shop talk."

He motioned to the server and she came to take SeaAnna's order. "Just black coffee, please."

Chris smiled. "Well, we can start there, I guess. I take mine black too. Always have."

"Me too," SeaAnna smiled back. "So, where should we start?" The coffee came quickly and she settled into the chair.

"I want to know all about you," said Chris. "Tell me as much or as little as you want. I'm sure Jo filled you in about me, as much as there is to tell. But I really do want to know about you."

And so, for the next three hours, almost until lunchtime, they talked. SeaAnna shared her recollections of growing up on the island, and she didn't hold back her resentment of being without a father. She discussed in detail the strained relationship between her and Susan which was only now starting to become more respectful and caring on her part. She spoke lovingly of Mike and proudly about Jo, indicating things had been rough there too.

"But it seems the end of summer brought about some mellowing for all of us," SeaAnna concluded. "And now we're feeling more like a family, I think, than ever before."

Chris was quiet for a few moments. "I guess finding out about me hasn't helped that family feeling much. I feel like an intruder in a way, although I swear I never had the first inkling of any of this. Certainly not about you."

"You know, I found that hard to believe at first," admitted SeaAnna. "But as time passed and I really thought about the world as it was all those years ago, I guess it does make sense that two people could completely fall out of communication with one another. You both could have tried a bit harder, and given each other the benefit of the doubt, but you didn't. It's a shame but there's not much we can do about that now."

"I have thought about that more than you can imagine, SeaAnna," Chris said. "That would never happen today with social media and Google and probably things I don't even know about. But you're right. We can't spend time on the what ifs. I can tell you it has brought me much joy to be in touch with Jo. Although our first meeting was more than a bit rocky."

SeaAnna laughed. "So she told me. But I'm grateful for her honesty when she figured out what was happening. And I think she has given us a good road map for where we go from here, don't you?"

Chris nodded his head in agreement. "It's been a process and it's been gradual and neither one of us has pushed. If that works for you, it works for me. I'd love to keep in touch, SeaAnna, even though I'll be back home and not here on the island. But it's not nineteen seventy-five so there are ways we can do that."

SeaAnna smiled. "Yes, thankfully there are. And I'd like that too. There are still things I'd like to know about you, but we've already kept this table for over three hours, so I think we'd better stop. Plus, I promised Mom I'd be home before lunch and at this rate I'll just make it."

Chris paid the bill at the counter, and they walked out together to her car. Chris felt it was too soon for a hug, but a handshake didn't seem right either. He reached out and took SeaAnna's hand in his.

"I'm so very honored to know I have a daughter like you,

SeaAnna. And proud. Thank you for this time together. I'll let you call or text whenever you feel like it. But please tell Mike I said hello. The few brief times we've met, I liked him. You know, I've now got a son-in-law too. I just hope in time, Susan will...."

His voice trailed off and SeaAnna clearly saw that he was hurting from Susan's actions.

"I think all three of us – me, Jo, and Mom – are pretty independent. And I'm sure you saw that in her even back then. Let's just keep hoping and giving her space."

"Right," he said. "Thanks again, and you take care. Drive safely tomorrow. It's going to be a bit of a blow but if you leave early, you should be OK."

SeaAnna smiled and waved goodbye as she left. She wanted so much to be able to tell her mom how it had gone, but knew that wouldn't be a good idea. Instead, she pulled over and jointly texted Mike and Jo.

It's early days but it went well. I can't believe I have a father. We've agreed to keep in touch. He's leaving the island next week. Back now to see Mom. Not expecting her to go along with seeing him but I sense she is questioning herself about her actions back in August. Just my gut feeling. Mike, I'm leaving early tomorrow so expect me about noon. Jo, I'll call when I get home. xo

Susan had lunch ready when Jo walked through the door. Her eyes were a bit puffy but SeaAnna refrained from asking any questions. Instead, she mentioned how hungry she was and that Susan's timing couldn't have been better. But Susan was nothing if not curious and insistent.

"So, are you going to tell me anything?" she asked.

"Um, I wasn't sure if you wanted to hear about this."

"I do," said Susan. "You and Jo have made your decisions and those choices one way or the other will impact me. I think I deserve to know."

SeaAnna placed her fork back on the table and looked at her mom. She saw her sadness and now a sense of isolation because of her choice. So, she carefully told Susan about her conversation with Chris and how they left things.

"It seems you like him, SeaAnna."

"Well, I don't dislike him, Mom. But it will take a lot of time and plenty more conversations to develop a real relationship with him. But you know, I can see why you fell for him. I really can. He's a nice man."

Susan burst into tears. "He was so wonderful, SeaAnna. He really was."

"He still is, Mom," SeaAnna said softly. "You need to just tear down those walls you've built and give the man a chance."

Chapter Fourteen

Dare was the happiest he'd been in a long time. As he drove along US 17 north from Charleston to Wilmington, he rehearsed over and over how he'd tell Jo the good news. He'd passed all the tests, and he could now apply for his captain's license. He had toyed with the idea of telling her he'd failed a portion of the exam, but he just couldn't do it. He was very proud of what he'd accomplished and he wanted her to be a part of his joy. He had already called his parents and Captain Jeff. They all expressed their congratulations and he knew when he got back on the island there would be a little celebration waiting, probably at Marcie's. He'd also texted Chris, who responded by letting him know he had never had any doubts.

It would take about five to seven weeks to get the actual license in hand, but it wasn't like he had a boat and he could immediately start taking on clients for fishing trips. His plan was to continue to mate for Captain Jeff and save up enough for a small deposit for a small boat of his own. He had a five-year timeline, which he felt made sense, and in those five years he would hone his skills as a mate. He'd also continue to watch Jeff closely to learn from him. Given Jeff's success, clearly Dare was learning from one of the best.

As he got closer to Jo, his excitement only grew.

It would be a great weekend. The timing of the conclusion of his exams coincided with the weekend that Jamie and the Hanks were doing an outdoor concert - the one Justyna had mentioned to Jo a few weeks back. When he asked Jo if she'd like to go, she readily agreed. In addition, Justyna along with Dare's friend Matthew were going to come too. Neither was familiar with the group, so Dare and Jo were anxious for them to hear their hometown celebrities. The weather was absolutely fall-like and it would be the perfect evening for a good seafood dinner with live music to follow.

They were all meeting at a local restaurant that Dare had visited before, so he knew how to get there and where to park. Dare asked Jo to come a few minutes early and she assumed it was because he had good news to share. Even though she knew Dare was absolutely prepared for the tests, she knew that you could never be sure how exams would go. Her own university experience had taught her that; however, no matter how difficult the test was, she always managed to come through it OK. She felt Dare would do the same.

As soon as she walked in and saw him sitting there with the biggest smile she'd ever seen him wear, she had her answer.

"So, may I sit here? It is Captain Dare now, I assume?" she laughed.

"It is, it is," he almost shouted. "Can you believe it, Jo? I did it. First time around."

"Of course, I believe it, Dare. Wow. So proud of you. What did your family say? I know you must have called them first thing."

"My mom was crying and I know Dad was happy. They know how much this meant to me. It's my future, after all. And I let Captain Jeff know. And Chris too. You know, he's really been helpful to me. He spent a lot of time with me before he left and we still keep in touch by text and all. How about you and Chris? Still OK?"

"Yes," said Jo. "And I have good news about Mom and Chris. After that initial meeting I told you about, they have texted back and forth several times and it seems to be going well. Mom says that they are finding things in common like foods they like and small stuff like that. But it's starting to build a bond. I can sense she is very happy about how it's working out."

"And your Gran? Is she still holding out talking to him again?"

"Unfortunately, yes. But Mom and Dad and I have decided to go to Hatteras for Thanksgiving, so Mom and I will have another talk with her. I think she's feeling a bit left out since obviously Mom and I are moving forward, but she says she can't But I won't give up on her. Not yet, anyway."

Jo looked up and saw her roommate walking in. "Hey, look who's here!"

Justyna walked in, and not a few minutes later, Matt arrived. There were handshakes and hugs all around in celebration of Dare's success. Drinks and food were ordered and the conversation was lively. When there was a lull, Jo cleared her throat.

"And I have some news for you, Dare, and for you too, Matt. I'm afraid Justyna already knows by virtue of her being my roommate. But I'm dying to share."

Dare looked up at her quizzically. "What have you not told me?"

"It's really just happened in the last few days, Dare. And I knew I'd see you this weekend. It's not a done deal or anything like that. But I can announce..." and she paused for dramatic effect.

"Oh, come on!" laughed Matt. "Out with it."

"Yours truly has been invited to apply for an honors term at the North Carolina Center for Aquatic Research in Belhaven for the fall semester! There were only two second year biology majors asked to apply. I'll get to really focus on my dear jellies. I'll do all my other classes for the term online. It's a bit of a dream come true for me. And I'll only be three hours away from the island instead of six. Which means, I'll be able to visit my grandmother much more regularly and I'll be that much closer to Mom and Dad in Raleigh."

"And you'll be three hours away from me," Justyna pretended to pout. "What will I do?" Then she jumped up and exclaimed, "Just kidding. I'm happy for you, Jo. And for you too, Dare. You two are really going after your dreams. Here's a toast!"

They clinked their glasses, enjoyed dinner, and made their way to the concert venue.

"Jo has talked non-stop about this group, Dare," said Justyna. "Can't wait to hear them."

"Me too," added Matthew. "I think Dare must be president of their fan club."

No one ended up being disappointed. The group played plenty of covers that all four of them recognized, and they sprinkled in a few of their own tunes which garnered plenty of applause from the audience. It was a high-energy performance.

"They really had a good turn out and they were great," said Jo as they walked out of the amphitheater. "It's good the weather was OK, otherwise we'd have been wet or cold or both. Playing at places like this will really get their name out there. Hope we don't lose them on the island!"

"They'd never stop playing at home," Dare said. "We gave them their start and I know both Jamie and his brother Hank – the older of the Hanks – and I think no matter how high their star rises, their feet will be firmly in Hatteras sand."

When they got to the dorm, Matthew and Dare said they were headed to Matthew's apartment for a few beers. Jo and Justyna said their goodbyes. Jo had an early morning of volunteering and Justyna was working on a paper.

"I'll see you at Thanksgiving then, Jo," said Dare. "And we'll have another celebration at Marcie's. That's our place."

"I think she is going to engrave plaques with our names on those two seats at the bar," chuckled Jo.

"And I hope that maybe you'll have luck with your Gran. I think she and Chris really would be an awesome couple."

"Me too, Dare. See you in just a few weeks."

But luck was not with Jo nor her family. A significant nor'easter reared its ugly head early in the week of Thanksgiving, and by Tuesday, the roads on Pea Island were flooded badly. Highway 12 was closed with no quick re-opening in sight as the swell continued. So, there would be no Thanksgiving with Susan this year.

SeaAnna, Jo, and Mike were very disappointed. Mike had actually been looking forward to the break from work even though it would only be about three days. And SeaAnna and Jo, although they hadn't talked to one another about it, were secretly hoping they could bring Susan around on the topic of Chris.

Chris called on Thanksgiving Day and Jo put him on speakerphone. He was spending the holiday with his nephew and his family, but wanted to be sure to talk to his "new family". Jo could hear kids in the back ground, football on the TV, and the murmur of conversations in the background.

"How many people are there, Chris?" Jo asked.

"Well, between Nate's own family and Candace's relatives who came, I think we have about twenty all together. It's pretty crazy as I'm sure you can hear."

"Have you shared with all of them about us?" asked SeaAnna. She hadn't wanted to ask him about his openness with his own family until now. Thanksgiving Day was such a family Day, so she felt maybe he'd broach the subject.

"Oh, SeaAnna, I should have let you know that I talked to them a long time ago. Right after I got back in town. I wasn't sure what the reaction would be, but I can tell you that they can't wait to meet you and Jo and Mike. I've told them about Susan as well, of course. Everyone's just hoping she'll change her mind. They want to meet her too and I'd like nothing more."

Neither SeaAnna nor Jo knew exactly how to respond to his comment about Susan.

"I think Jo and I both were thinking about talking to her during this visit, but since we aren't there, it won't be as easy," said SeaAnna. "We're going to call her in just a bit. We'll have to see how it goes."

"Fair enough," said Chris. "They're calling me to dinner now, so you all take care, and Jo, congratulations again on the honor term nomination you texted me about. I'm proud of you."

Once they had ended the call, SeaAnna looked at Mike and said, "He didn't mention Christmas. I don't know what to make of that."

Mike looked at both SeaAnna and Jo. "I don't think either of you should make anything of it. He's probably not even thinking of Christmas. Most men don't operate that way. One holiday at a time. Just be thankful. It is Thanksgiving. Think about how far you've both come in a short period of time. Remember last year's Thanksgiving? We never could have imagined this. As I recall the two of you barely spoke. So, we do have plenty to be thankful for. But now I think we need to video chat with Susan. I'm hoping she managed to cook a nice dinner."

Susan answered immediately and Jo suspected she'd had her phone right next to her, expecting their call.

"Hey Gran," said Jo as Susan came into view.

"Hi Mom," added SeaAnna. "Happy Thanksgiving from all of us. Wave, Mike."

Mike dutifully waved and wished Susan well. "I'm going to relax on my recliner and watch some football, Susan. I know you girls want to talk."

Jo noticed that her grandmother seemed a bit pale, and SeaAnna asked her if she'd lost weight.

"I guess a little," Susan admitted. "Without you and Mike or Jo here, I'm just not cooking as much. And I've been walking every day on the beach, so I'm sure that's helping."

"Walking is good," said Jo. "What did you have today for Thanksgiving dinner?"

"The neighbors brought me over a huge plate of food. I'll probably eat off it for days. I missed your turkey and dressing and all, SeaAnna. "

"I know, Mom. We're missing you too. Overwash is the one really tough thing about the island. But hey, did Jo tell you her news?"

Jo nodded. "I texted her this morning. What do you think, Gran?"

"What do I think? I think it's marvelous, Jo. For a lot of reasons, but mostly because you're following your dream. And if it comes to pass, it will be nice to have you that much closer."

They talked a little longer, but there didn't seem to be an opening to bring up the previous conversation with Chris. Susan brought up Christmas and said she was hopeful they could get together on the island.

"I thought we'd have Christmas here in Raleigh, Mom, but I'll talk to Mike. We'll think about it. Never had a big island Christmas," SeaAnna said. Jo was surprised. Christmas in Raleigh was pretty much a given, so this change in attitude was amazing. So much to be thankful for.

"My break starts on the nineteenth of December, Gran. We'll get back to you with our plans, OK?" Jo asked.

"Absolutely," said Susan. "I do hope y'all will seriously consider coming here."

SeaAnna and Jo nodded in agreement and blew kisses as they said goodbye.

Immediately, Jo's ringtone began. It was Dare. She stepped into the kitchen to take the call.

"Hi Jo. Happy Thanksgiving to you and your family. It sucks that you couldn't make it. Is your Gran OK?"

"We just now had a video chat with her. She's fine. Just really disappointed. I hope you're having a good day."

"I am. We all ate too much. Now everyone's half asleep watching football. But I wanted to put something out there for you and your mom and dad. You can talk about it while you're all together. I know you always spend Christmas in Raleigh, but this year they're doing something new at the docks right before Christmas and I thought maybe y'all could come here."

"Hold on, Dare, let me put you on speakerphone and get to my folks."

She wandered into the living room and turned the TV on mute. She indicated it was Dare on the phone.

"OK, Dare, what is it?" Jo asked.

"Happy Thanksgiving, Mr. and Mrs. Leonard. I was just telling Jo that there's going to be a new Christmas event this year on the island. It's going to be a festival of lights with all the charter boats at the docks. They're planning music and food and it just sounds like a great time. It would be awesome if you could come and maybe spend Christmas on the island this year. Bring Miss Susan too, of course. Would you think about it?"

Mike said, "I think it's a great idea. It would definitely be something new and I think Susan would be absolutely thrilled. Time for a change in our routine."

SeaAnna was nodding slowly. "I never thought I would want to, but we were just talking about Christmas plans and it all seems to be coming together. Sure, Dare. We'll come. I assume Captain Terry's boat will be all decked out?"

"Oh, for sure. Everyone's talking about it. After the storm and all, it just seems like a good thing to do. That's great news. Let's just hope we have better weather. It will be great to see you, Mr. and Mrs. Leonard. And Jo, we'll have that celebratory dinner at Marcie's, for sure."

Jo talked to Dare a while longer, and then ended the conversation.

"Wow, Mom, I'm glad you went with the idea," said Jo. "And Dad, you really seem to be into it. A family Christmas on the island. Well, almost the whole family."

SeaAnna smiled. "Yes, almost the whole family but let's take what we have and make the most of it."

As SeaAnna and Jo walked back into the kitchen together for a little more pumpkin pie, Mike leaned back on his recliner and smiled to himself.

Christmas, he thought. *A time for surprises.*

Chapter Fifteen

Jo and SeaAnna seemed almost giddy on the drive from Raleigh to Hatteras. Mike concentrated on driving and let the two of them talk seemingly incessantly for the majority of the four-hour trip. One thing mother and daughter had always had in common, despite their differences, was a love of the Christmas season. With so many positive things happening in their family, it seemed like this Christmas would really be one to remember.

Jo had driven from Wilmington as soon as her final exam ended. Mike and SeaAnna already had their car packed so when she arrived, they loaded up her suitcase and gifts, and they headed off. Susan was expecting them for dinner and Jo honestly couldn't wait. She hadn't seen her grandmother since she'd left in September. Video chatting was a wonderful part of technology but it just couldn't replace the real thing. Everyone had certainly learned that from the pandemic.

"I guess I am a bit sad we won't see Chris at Christmas," Jo said. "But at least he said he'd try to come to Raleigh before I have to go back to school."

"I know," said SeaAnna. "I had hoped we'd all be together but I think he didn't feel right being on the island knowing he couldn't see Mom. In Raleigh that pressure won't be there and we can just enjoy ourselves. Plus, he'll be with his extended family for Christmas so I think it works out OK for now."

"He's thoughtful, and more patient than I am, for sure," said Jo. "It's pretty cool how close we've become this fall. And you too, Mom. Boy, when we thought about our 'bingo cards' for this year at the end of last year, we sure didn't figure on 'meeting long lost father and grandfather'."

"I'd agree with that," said Mike. "I don't know if you two chatterboxes realize it but we are just about thirty minutes away. How about some Christmas music that I can actually hear for this last bit of the drive?"

SeaAnna reached over and turned up the volume on the satellite holiday channel and they all got lost in their own pleasant thoughts until they turned into Susan's drive. She was waiting for them on the porch, wearing a light coat as the weather was seasonably cool but not terribly cold. It would be perfect for the Holiday Festival of Lights the next evening.

Jo bounded out of the car and took the steps two at a time.

"Merry Christmas, Gran! I'm so happy to be here. You look great. Lots of color in your cheeks so you must be walking every day."

Susan hugged Jo tightly. "Yes, I have been. I never had another problem with my ankle and it's so beautiful on the beach right now."

"We'll definitely be taking some walks together, all of us," said Jo.

By then SeaAnna had made it to the top of the stairs and greeted her mother warmly.

"It's good to be here, Mom. Having a Hatteras Christmas will be special. Have you bought a tree? Mike brought some decorations from home so we can add to yours and make it a real family tree so to speak."

Mike was lugging up the suitcases and Jo offered to run back down and help him with the mountain of gifts they all had brought - not just for Susan but also for each other. They planned to stay through Christmas Day and head back the day after Christmas. That gave them a full week. Jo hoped time would just slow down now so she could savor each moment.

"Gran, are you excited about the Festival of Lights? Dare's been telling me about all the preparations and I think Captain Jeff is going to allow him to co-pilot the *Carefree* with him in the boat parade. It should be amazing and the weather is going to cooperate. At least no rain."

"Ah, I'm not sure I'm going," said Susan. She had moved into the kitchen and had her back to them at the sink where she was opening a bottle of wine.

"What?" said SeaAnna "You know that was a big part

of our coming here. At least coming this early. Why don't you want to go?"

"Not sure," said Susan sadly. "This is going to be a great Christmas with the three of you here, but..."

"But what? I don't get it," lamented Jo. "You'll change your mind tomorrow when we're all getting ready. We'll have an early dinner at Marcie's and you'll be fine. Promise me you'll think about it. Please?"

Susan gave them all a weak smile. "Sure, I'll think about it."

After dinner, as Jo and SeaAnna did the dishes, she saw her dad take Susan aside.

"It would really be great if you'd come with us, Susan," she heard him say. "I don't know what's bothering you, but just set it aside tomorrow, and we'll have a good time. It's Christmas after all and we did miss out on Thanksgiving."

"OK, Mike," Susan replied as she gave him a hug. "Thanks for talking sense into me. Sometimes I just get in a mood. The festival is going to be very special, from what I've heard, and we're going to have fun. Now let's have a bit more wine and finish decorating the tree."

Susan seemed to relax then, and they spent the evening decorating, listening to Christmas music, and laughing more than any of them could remember.

The next morning dawned crisp and clear. Jo had texted Dare to see if they could get together, but he said he'd be tied up helping out at the docks all day and he'd see her that evening.

After breakfast, Jo announced they'd all be taking a good walk along the beach. It was low tide in an hour or so and the beach would be nice and flat. Susan and SeaAnna got their coats and hats, but Mike said for them to go on. He'd wait for them and maybe even try to fix them lunch.

He had some work to finish up on, and he wanted to rest from the drive yesterday.

"Does Dad seem preoccupied to you?" Jo asked SeaAnna as they started walking. "Oh, he's always that way at the end of the year. I guess clients have all kinds of year-end questions and your dad feels obligated to help them out. He's good like that."

Jo then turned to Susan. "Are you all over the bit of blues you had last night, Gran? You look more chipper today. Hey, what should we all wear tonight? Christmas sweaters or something a bit more more tame?"

In the end, they all decided coats and hats were again in order, as the temperature was expected to drop fairly substantially during the evening. The skies were perfectly clear and there was no moon, so the starts were out in abundance as soon as the sun set. As they pulled up to the docks, they realized they were lucky to find a parking place. It seemed most everyone on the island had come for this inaugural celebration.

All three women stepped out of the car and looked around. There were lights strung everywhere, on every piling and from building to building. Christmas music was coming from speakers placed strategically along the walkways. Jo knew Jamie and the Hanks would play later, but there was still about an hour before things really got started. The smells of the oyster roast were incredibly tantalizing and Jo was thankful they'd eaten before they came. Otherwise, she could have easily eaten every oyster there.

"Wow, this is really magical," Jo said softly. "It's just so different from how we always see it in the summer."

"Yes, it is lovely," agreed Susan. "What do you think, SeaAnna?"

"Honestly, I'm impressed," she said. "I had no idea it

would be this big of a deal. But what do we do now? Where are we supposed to go?"

Mike inserted himself into the conversation. "I think we should walk to the far end of the dock. That's where the boat line up will be. Dare texted me today while y'all were walking. He said that would be best."

Jo thought it was a bit unusual that Dare had texted Mike, but then they had been in touch more often recently, Mike had said. It also seemed they were walking away from where most of the spectators were, but perhaps the organizers expected even more of a crowd and this way Jo and her family would have a good vantage point.

"Hot chocolates, anyone?" Mike asked. Three hands shot up. "I'll be right back, then. Don't move because I don't want to lose you."

As they stood there, they noticed most of the boats were already getting in some sort of line up. Jo still hadn't seen the *Carefree* or Dare. Then, as Mike arrived with their hot drinks, he motioned for them to look up.

There, coming around the corner, was a small boat all festooned in twinkling lights. It looked new. Jo guessed about twenty feet, but it did have a little tuna tower, as the captain's lookout were known. *Good for sound fishing*, she thought. And then she gasped.

"Oh my God, look! It's Dare. What in the world?"

SeaAnna stood fixated at the sight of the small craft coming up beside them. There on the side was the name of the boat, the *SeaAnna II*.

Susan felt faint and grabbed Jo's arm. Dare was smiling and waving from the tower. SeaAnna was crying but she wasn't sure why.

Dare climbed down and Mike helped him moor the boat to the pilings. "Welcome aboard!" Dare shouted.

Jo climbed onto the deck. "Dare, where did you get this boat? How, when...?"

"Ask your dad," Dare grinned.

"Dad, Mike?" the three women said in unison.

"Well, it's a long story but it's not," he said as he helped SeaAnna and Susan onboard. "Captain Jeff and Chris have been keeping in touch all fall, and you know I keep in touch with Chris from time to time. When Dare passed his exam and got his license, which he now has in hand..." They looked up and Dare waved a piece of paper proudly. "We decided to help him out a bit," Mike continued. "Jeff said he was ready to expand his business a bit, and in his opinion, Dare was ready to have a boat of his own. We all pitched in. Dare will be paying us back over time. He's earned it and I have no doubts he'll make us all whole in no time."

"But, Dare," Jo said. "How could you not tell me?"

"I didn't know until a few days ago," said Dare. "Honestly. And once I did know, I was sworn to secrecy." He looked to Mike for support.

"It's true. Jeff took care of things from this end and only picked up the boat a few days ago and brought it down. He lucked out in that someone had ordered this boat and then cancelled, so he was able to get it pretty quickly."

"And the name?" asked SeaAnna through her tears. "I'm overwhelmed."

"Captain Jeff said that when they lost the first *SeaAnna* in Hurricane Evelyn, he'd always hoped to have another one in tribute to his Uncle Terry. The *Carefree* was already named when he bought it, so here she is, the *SeaAnna II.*"

"This is just wonderful," clapped Susan as she regained her composure. "Dare, I'm proud of you and, Mike, thank you for your part. Dare certainly deserves this, as hard

working as he is. And good for Jeff for stepping up too."
Everyone noticed she had omitted any mention of Chris.

"So, we'll be in the parade now on this boat?" Jo asked.

"That's the idea," said Dare. "I had your dad have you
walk down here so you could have the surprise and get on
board before I had to get in the line-up."

Jo looked askance at Mike who smiled sheepishly.
"Work? You didn't have work today," she laughed. "You've
been scheming, Dad."

"Guilty as charged," said Mike. "Now, where do you
want us all, Dare?"

"Jo, come up on the tower with me. Mr. and Mrs.
Leonard why don't you go up front by the bow? Miss Susan,
you can sit on the seat on the stern."

"Shouldn't we be going soon?" asked Jo once she had
clamored up the few steps to the tower.

"Ah, we've got one more passenger, I think," said Dare.
"And if I'm not mistaken, that's him now."

Jo looked to where Dare was pointing. She saw an older
man, half walking half running, toward them. Then she put
her hand over her mouth and closed her eyes for a second. It
was Chris. And this, she realized, was a set-up.

From their vantage point, Mike and SeaAnna saw him
too. SeaAnna felt like everything was moving in slow
motion. She realized, as Jo had, that this had been planned
ahead of time. Mike winked at her.

"Permission to board, sir," Chris smiled, hollering up at
Dare.

"Permission granted. Welcome!"

Chris jumped on board and nodded to SeaAnna and Jo.
Then he turned to Susan. Her face was unreadable but she
didn't make a move to disembark. Dare took no time in
asking Chris to jump back off and loosen the ropes. He

jumped back on deftly. He hadn't been a mate for all those years without knowing his way around a boat and dock.

Dare maneuvered the *SeaAnna II* out of her parking spot and into the channel to join the parade. Chris looked down at Susan.

"May I sit here, Susan?" he asked gently. She said nothing but slid slightly to the side to make a little more room.

SeaAnna wanted to look back at her mom in the worst way but Mike took her hand and whispered, "Let whatever is going to happen, happen, SeaAnna dear."

She put her head on his shoulder and kept her eyes on the beautiful view of all the boats gathering now to parade by the docks and the large crowd. Jamie and the Hanks were valiantly belting out some Christmas carols.

Jo had the same view from up above and willed herself not look at her grandmother. She spoke to Dare as quietly as she could, "You knew about Chris coming, didn't you?"

Dare nodded solemnly, afraid of her response.

"Thank you," was all she said.

The boats were all moving in the procession now and the music and the lights all melded into an incredibly beautiful panorama. It was Christmastime, for sure.

Chris looked at Susan and said as softly as he could so that no one else could hear, "Susan, I want to say again how sorry I am. Truly. I miss you. It's been an incredible thing in my life to find SeaAnna and Jo, but mostly to find you again. You're everything to me. I love you, Susan."

He moved to place his hand over hers, and she didn't pull it away.

"Please give me a second chance. Give *us* a chance," he pleaded.

Susan looked up and saw a sparkle in his eyes. It could

have been the reflection of the lights dancing on the water, or from the stars in the sky. But Susan knew better. She'd seen that sparkle before, and she knew what she needed to do. It was finally what she wanted to do. She leaned into Chris and put her hand over his and whispered, "Yes, I'll try. Let's give us a chance. I love you too."

Epilogue

Chris and Susan did give it a chance, and they were very successful. Chris sold his business to his nephew the following spring and moved into a month-to-month rental not far from the docks. Susan worked with Mike and SeaAnna to sell the motel. Susan and Chris spent days and hours walking along the beach, cooking for one another, making up for lost time, and spending more time at Susan's than at his little cottage. Almost a year to the date of Hurricane Eva, Chris dropped to one knee on the beach one lovely afternoon and proposed. Susan tearfully accepted and their wedding was one of the island's highlights of the fall. They planned it over fall break so Jo could be there, and the newlyweds made their get-away on the *SeaAnna II*.

Mike started to plan his retirement and surprised SeaAnna by suggesting they buy a second home on the island. Even more surprising to her was the fact that he'd come to love fishing.

He, Dare, and Chris spent many days when Dare didn't have a charter fishing in the sound and even a few times in the ocean. Chris also taught Mike a thing or two about surf fishing, and in a word, Mike was hooked. SeaAnna began to enjoy her time on the island more and more, and found solace in appreciating her roots. Her relationship with Chris began to blossom and while she still couldn't bring herself to call him dad, she figured, as did he, what was in the heart of the person talking to you was more important than what you might be called.

Jo was accepted for the honor term and planned to re-apply for a second term as soon as she could. She loved her studies, but even more, she loved being closer to the island. She settled into a loving and supportive granddaughter-grandfather relationship with Chris, and that pleased Susan immensely. As for she and Dare, they remained the very best of friends. Shrimp baskets at Marcie's and going to hear Jamie and the Hanks play at the docks were absolutes when she was on the island.

And what about Jamie and the Hanks? Well, the band just kept on playing. Resilient they were, just like the islanders and their beloved island.

* * *

Storm Season

Storm Season

There's something about laughing in the dunes,
And shadows dancing wildly in the full moon –
Can I be feeling this so soon?
I think I really love you.
The tides can come and go,
The winds just blow and blow –
By now I think you know,
How much I really love you.
The storm season blew us apart,
I know I broke your heart.
Please give me a chance at a new start –
You know I'll always love you.

By Jamie and the Hanks
Puppy Drum Music
Words by Jamie Littleton
Music by Hank Littleton and Hank Neff

Thank you so much for reading Storm Season. Follow Jan on Facebook for Outer Banks photos, author updates, and information on upcoming books. https://www.facebook.com/JanetMDawsonWriter/

Acknowledgments

I never thought I'd write a novel. It wasn't on my bucket list, not on my list of things to do when I retired. But once the story line came to me, I couldn't seem to get it out of my mind.

After hearing me talk about it for the umpteenth time, my husband asked me when was I going to sit down and actually put the story into writing?

I am an avid reader, and so I have read many acknowledgment sections. It really does take a team of supporters to get you through the process. The writing is just the beginning.

I want to thank my brother, Weather Channel meteorologist Jeff Morrow, for his insights on forecasting back in the 70s, and for helping me understand how tropical forecasting has changed over the decades.

My neighbor John Hooper helped me understand the process of obtaining a "6 Pack" captain's license, which is the license most charter captains hold.

My squad of friends and family who gave me encouragement as I went chapter by chapter included N.P. Littleton, Susan Keller, Sandra Dawson, Jenni Enqvist, Candace Mastel, Lisa Morrow, Emily Morrow, Erin Morrow, Carolyn Vallecorsa, MaryAnn Vallecorsa, and Lisa Woodis along with our island's local bookseller and local author cheerleader Gee Gee Rosell.

My massage therapist Robin Kukiel connected me with

author Kim Perry who held my hand through the entire editing and publishing process. She also designed the fantastic cover which features our ubiquitous island flower, the JoBell. My editor Vanda O'Neill cleaned up my manuscript in ways I never dreamed possible!

My teachers - from Susan Corsi Sullivan in second grade, to my high school English teacher, Karen Finnerty. I was blessed to have many teachers who encouraged my love of reading and writing. From my first attempts at poetry and story writing as a little girl, to my class papers on favorite authors and my work on the high school paper and year-book, they led me to believe I could do and be whatever I wanted. And certainly my parents, Clifford and Dolores Morrow, who introduced me to the Outer Banks all those years ago, did the same with parental love, encouragement, and guidance.

In a strange way, I owe Hurricanes Matthew and Dorian my thanks for giving me the real-life experience with hurricanes and hurricane resiliency on Hatteras Island.

And last, but not certainly not least, I thank my husband, Dave. His gentle prodding kept me working on the manuscript many times when I thought I'd just let it go. Our walks on the beach brought me clarity and many new ideas. His 52 years of motel ownership at the Cape Hatteras Motel certainly provided plenty of background for the Hatteras Hideaway in this novel.

Our marriage is proof that you can have a second chance at a good thing!

About the Author

Jan Morrow Dawson began visiting the Outer Banks with her family in 1964. She has had previous careers in marketing and public relations, in broadcast journalism, and in the non-profit sector through the local, national and international YMCA movements. In 2005 she did humanitarian work in Kosovo with the United Methodist Committee on Relief.

When she returned to Hatteras in 2015 to care for her mother, she reconnected with her old beach boyfriend after a 40-plus year separation and they married in 2016. She spent eight years in the hospitality business at the Cape Hatteras Motel doing everything from laundry to handling the front desk to social media. Now both retired from the motel business, the Dawsons reside in Buxton on Hatteras Island in the home her parents built. Storm Season is her first novel.

If you'd like to connect, follow her on Facebook for Outer Banks photos, author updates, and information on upcoming books. https://www.facebook.com/JanetMDawsonWriter/

Made in the USA
Columbia, SC
28 April 2025

57254030R00102